MW00964121

To Kate,

I am eternally humbled by the kindness you have shown me as I fumbled into my writing career. I could not be prouder to call you my mentor, my friend, and my fellow writer.

With warmest thoughts always,

Eden Baylee

fall into winter

four erotic novellas
eden baylee

iUniverse, Inc.
Bloomington

Fall into Winter
Four Erotic Novellas

iUniverse books may be ordered through booksellers or by contacting:

iUniverse
1663 Liberty Drive
Bloomington, IN 47403
www.iuniverse.com
1-800-Authors (1-800-288-4677)

Cover design by John Beadle.

Cover photographs courtesy of iStockphoto.

ISBN: 978-1-4502-7824-9 (sc)
ISBN: 978-1-4502-7825-6 (dj)
ISBN: 978-1-4502-7826-3 (ebook)

Library of Congress Control Number: 2010918788

Printed in the United States of America

iUniverse rev. date: 12/17/2010

For my husband, who makes it all possible

contents

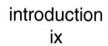

introduction

When I set out to write my first book of erotic fiction, it came after a lengthy period of introspection, indecision, and intimidation. Intimidation, you ask? Of what … or by whom?

Many people dream of quitting their day jobs to pursue different paths. I was one of them, and my dream was to write. After more than thirty years of writing for my own pleasure, I took the leap to doing it full time. I could no longer meet the demands on my left brain during the day and expect to have anything of creative value for my right brain at night. When I finally made the decision to leave my job, it was surprising how *right* it felt.

Of course, when giving up something secure and familiar to follow a dream, there are consequences. I suppose that's what I meant by *intimidation*. There's something quite intimidating about those damn consequences! The thoughts of failure, looking foolish, or not being able to support oneself are only the obvious ones. *I* was the one who had intimidated myself out of pursuing a life as a writer, and now I had to embrace it. But what of this life? Could it be as easy as waking up and writing every day, and was it possible for me to work in isolation and be so disciplined? For now, I am happy to say yes, but one book does not a writer make. At least not in my books—pun intended. Time will tell.

Erotica has been part of my library since before I reached puberty, so it's no surprise it left an indelible mark on my psyche. Don't ask me how I got away with reading such stuff as a kid—I just did. I'm sure it's why I have always had an active fantasy life—one I now intend to share with you through my writing. Much of the inspiration for my book began as sparks from past experiences, but there also exists a huge element from mundane events. The simplest things can be so sensual. I encourage you to consider that when you go about your daily life—getting dressed to go out, drinking a glass of water, or engaging in conversation with a stranger. It's my belief that everyday life is rich with the seeds for erotica when we are in tune with our bodies and minds.

Fall into Winter is a collection of four tales designed to stimulate and heighten your senses. Though common elements unify the stories, each one is unique and stands alone—feel free to read them out of order. With plenty of sex to tie the plots and characters together, my hope is that these stories will make you feel sensuous and sexier for having read them.

Re-creating oneself is never easy; however, I've been able to do it with the help of some amazing people in my life. You're the ones I've stayed in touch with and go to for support, whose advice I value, and who I'm proud to include in my circle of family and friends. It is encouraging to see this circle grow wider with each passing season.

The one person who deserves special mention is the man who inspires me daily with his own creative spirit. I am now, and will forever be, in your debt.

Stay sexy,
Eden Baylee

fall

seduced by the blues

Ella Jamieson took a sip of her scotch and glanced over at the man to her left. They stood at the bar of X-tasy, the newest nightclub in town. It was billed as the next hot spot in New York since Marquee went under a few months ago, and Ella had received comps for the club's opening night. It was a Saturday evening in October, and the weather was starting to cool off after a sweltering summer. She had taken in the scene for the past hour and was just about to leave when he walked up beside her. It had been boring up to that point, and she craved some excitement. For some reason, the young man standing next to her made her feel particularly wicked.

"Did you come here to get laid?" she asked, not even looking in his direction, though it was obvious her question was intended for no one else.

"Pardon me?" He turned to her—his eyes narrowing to focus in the dark room.

"I asked if you came here to get laid."

"I don't know what you mean."

The music was loud, and she knew he was having difficulty hearing her. She moved to face him. "I mean, I hope you're not here for the music."

"Why, what's wrong with it?" he asked.

"Nothing's wrong, but you can't call this music—a DJ playing shitty remixes of eighties' hits is just bad."

"This isn't an eighties song."

1

She heard defiance in his voice and immediately felt aroused. "How much do you want to bet?"

"What are we betting for?"

"A drink." Ella sipped the last of her scotch.

"Deal."

They shook on it, and now Ella took a long hard look at him. She guessed him to be in his midtwenties, probably still in diapers when this song came out. He was cute, though—definitely her type—boyish, tall, and lean.

Over the last few decades, some of the best music from the sixties and seventies were sampled and remixed in clubs. She didn't even include eighties music, as disco had already sucked a lot of originality out of that era, being the decade littered with one-hit wonders. Ella felt there was so little originality in any of the new music released today, and with few exceptions, most artists had no staying power. She much preferred the music of earlier generations.

"Do you even *know* this song?" she asked.

"No, but I'm looking it up on my iPhone. Tell you in a sec."

"Don't bother. It's called 'Everything She Wants.'"

He glared at her with his baby blues. "How'd you know that?"

"I've been around music for a while."

He fidgeted with his phone, inputting her information.

"Trust me," she said, amused he wasn't taking her word for it. "I'm right. The song is by Wham."

"Shit, you *are* right. 'Everything She Wants' came out in nineteen eighty-five."

"Yes, so why are we listening to a bad remix of a twenty-five-year-old song?"

"You have a point."

The bartender came by, and she ordered a double. "He's paying," she said, nodding in her young man's direction. She turned and walked to a nearby table.

She could tell he was intrigued—they usually were. At thirty-eight, she had been on the singles' scene for longer than she cared to remember and was resigned to staying that way. Ella stood five feet seven with heels and had the supple, slim body of a woman in her midtwenties. Her curly auburn hair fell just below her shoulders, highlighting her dark brown eyes. Tonight, she wore a black lambskin pencil skirt with a slit up the back and a matching jacket.

She loved leather and wore it often in the fall. It made her feel powerful and seductive. Underneath, she was dressed only in red silk lingerie. Her bare legs were exposed, wearing a pair of scarlet pumps.

Working as a promoter for a rock radio station had provided her with plenty of opportunities to go to clubs, but the hours had meant other areas of her life had suffered. Though she met many men, and suspected she had more sex than any of her married girlfriends did, finding that special someone had eluded her.

He brought their drinks and sat down next to her. "So … are you here on your own?"

"Yes."

"My name's John."

"I'm Ella. Nice to meet you, John."

"Ella? Named after the 'First Lady of Song'?"

"If you mean Ella Fitzgerald, that's right. You're familiar with her music?"

"I dabble in jazz. Are you a fan?"

"Not at all. Classic rock is my specialty."

Just then, a remix of David Bowie's 1983 hit "China Girl" came on.

"Another eighties song?" he asked.

"Yes, do you want to bet again?"

"No, no, I get the feeling I'm out of my league here."

A sense of humor, polite, and cute—he was definitely fuckable material. Aside from his messy mop of dark brown hair, he was extremely clean-cut. He wore a light dress shirt with a jacket and black jeans. She guessed him to be some Wall Street banker, possibly a lawyer, less likely an accountant. He appeared well built and obviously went to the gym—that was a given. Like most of the men she met who enjoyed coming to the clubs, he probably didn't have a clue about music prior to the nineties. By contrast, Ella grew up in the seventies with two older siblings. From early on, she was immersed in the British Invasion and Motown, and she had a collection of vinyl that would probably make her seem ancient to someone John's age.

"So, John, how did you get into this place?"

"I came with a friend, but he had to leave early. You?"

"I'm on the job."

"Oh? What do you do?"

"Radio promoter."

"Aha! No wonder you know so much about music. You must have taken me for a sucker right away."

No, she didn't, but she wouldn't mind being sucked by him.

"Actually, that's not true," she said. "I got into radio because of my interest in music, not the other way around."

"Still, I'm not sure our bet was made in good faith. You had an unfair advantage."

"Yes, I did, but that's the nature of making a bet, isn't it? I'm not required to disclose all the facts."

"Okay, how about you give me a chance to even things up?"

"What did you have in mind?" Ella was always up for a flirtatious sparring match.

"Now that I know what you do, how about you guess what I do for a living? If you're wrong, you buy the next round."

"And if I'm right?"

"I don't think you'll be right."

He was cocky, something she attributed to his young age. She guessed he had no idea how old she was.

"Okay John, you're on. How many guesses do I get?"

"I'll be a gentleman and give you two."

"Very generous of you." She went with her gut instinct. "My guess is you're a banker."

"Nope," he said, smirking.

"All right, then ... a lawyer."

He eyed her with defeat, but only for a second before he let out an exuberant laugh. "The lady's getting the next round!"

Ella was shocked. It was rare she was wrong about these things, having had ample experience with younger men. John was sly—she had to give him that.

"Give me one more guess." She hated to lose.

"Okay, but you're still buying me a drink."

"All right, all right." She liked that he didn't give in to her. "I almost said this as my second choice—an accountant."

"Survey says ... so sorry!"

"Damn!" she said.

John motioned for the waitress. "I'll have a vodka martini with a twist please." He looked over to Ella. "And another double scotch for the lady—neat, right?"

"Yes, thanks. I need it." Ella was having fun despite losing the bet.

The noise of the club suddenly became unbearable with the Britney Spears version of Joan Jett and the Blackhearts' "I Love Rock 'n Roll." That was about all she could take. When X-tasy billed itself as the next big club with a retro feel, she had thought she would be listening to some old classics, not bad remakes of them.

"It's getting louder in here, if that's even possible," he yelled into her ear.

Ella found the perfect opening for her next move. "I know. Let's leave after this drink."

*   *   *   *

They hailed a cab to Madame Z, an established bar and lounge club she had frequented in her twenties—John suggested it. She heard it was turned into a jazz and blues club several years ago, but the name had remained.

"Exactly how old are you?" she asked him in the cab.

"Twenty-six. Why?"

"Just curious. I didn't think you would know of Madame Z. It's a bit old for you, isn't it?"

"I have eclectic tastes—that includes my music."

"Really? And what else?"

"Women," he said, staring straight at her. She felt her pussy flutter and found him quite adorable.

"So, John, are you going to tell me what you do?"

"No, I want to keep you guessing." He was a flirt—and a very good one at that.

It was close to ten thirty when they arrived at the club, and she was beginning to feel the effects of the drinks she had. When they got out of the cab, she casually glanced at who the headliner was for the coming week and saw a poster of John on the front window. It read JOHN COOK—BLUES GUITARIST. SELECTED EVENING SHOWS.

"What's this?" She turned to him, her mouth agape.

"Just something I do when I'm not playing a banker or a lawyer."

"You're performing here?"

"I wouldn't believe everything you read. Just because the sign says …"

Ella punched him on the shoulder. "Damn it! You led me to think you knew nothing about music, and you're a bloody musician!"

He laughed loudly and guided her into the club. "Ella, you never asked, and I didn't lead you on. True, I may not be familiar with rock or pop music, but there's probably little about jazz and blues I don't know."

Ella had to admit this was the biggest surprise she'd had in a long time.

"You've played here before?"

"Once or twice."

"Everyone seemed to know you when we came in."

"One of the perks of being part owner."

"Really?" Ella was impressed, and that didn't happen often, certainly not when it came to younger men and what they did for a living.

John brought her upstairs to his private office, and they sat facing each other on a plush, velvety red couch. Ella surveyed the surroundings and found the room functional and cozy. The lighting was dim and the decor contemporary. There was a desk with a computer on it, and a stand with three guitars in the corner. The walls were bare except for a large black-and-white print of John Lee Hooker. The room had a sexy vibe to it, and it was comfortable—too much so. She couldn't remember the last time a man took charge with her, almost forgetting that *she* had intended to make the conquest. For someone only in his twenties, he had an air of sophistication she had never encountered.

"Do you bring all your young women here?"

John looked at her seriously with his pale blue eyes. "I don't bring women here. This is where I work."

"Oh, so you brought me up here for business?"

"No, but sometimes it's good to mix business with pleasure."

She liked how he played with words. His calm intelligence turned her on.

"Why me, then?"

"I liked you from the moment I saw you, and when you asked me if I was at X-tasy to get laid … I must admit, I found that impossible to resist."

Ella now felt embarrassed for saying it. "That was pretty forward of me."

"Yes, it was, and to answer your question … I didn't go there to get laid, but the night is still young."

He leaned in to kiss her. Though she was used to being in control, she thought she might give up some of it—just for tonight.

He licked around her mouth and gently bit her lips. She liked that he was in no hurry. With his fingers tangled in her curls, John drew her in. Ella met his tongue with hers, wrestling with it and tasting the smoky-sweet combination of his martini and her scotch. He cradled her back and nuzzled behind her ears, sending chills up her spine. It didn't take her long to feel hot moisture seep between her slit.

At that moment, she decided she had to have more of him and got up from the couch. Removing her jacket and hiking up her skirt, she sat on John's lap facing him, kneeling with her calves spread out on either side of his thighs. She could tell he was surprised by her aggressiveness, but he was obviously turned on—the bulge in his pants proved it. Ella thrust against him in an erotic grinding motion. He groaned, and she pressed her lips on top of his. They battled inside each other's mouths. John held her ass while she gyrated. He slipped his right hand down the front of her panties.

"Damn. Ella, you're dripping."

He penetrated her with his middle finger. She rode him and felt another inserted into her as his thumb worked its magic on her clit. He slid a hand underneath her bra, grasping her left breast. He squeezed till she moaned. Her nipples were already stiff when he pinched them.

Ella arched backward as John thrilled her by tonguing between her cleavage. She felt him growing bigger as she pushed her pussy toward him. Her breathing became labored as he continued to play with her. She shut her eyes and dug her nails into his shoulders—she was close.

"John, you're up in fifteen!" yelled a voice from outside the door.

Ella froze.

"Okay, Bill," he said. "I'll be right there." His voice was composed.

"Shit! You're performing *tonight*?" she asked in a hushed tone.

"Yup, in fifteen, like the man said."

"You have to go." Ella moved to get off him.

"No, no, not yet." He didn't stop touching her for a second. "We have a little pleasure to take care of first." John resumed stroking her in the same unhurried manner as before. Soon she felt the heat building again in her groin.

Ella held onto his shoulders and adjusted her position to allow his thumb more room to vibrate her swollen bud. She was amazed at how agile his fingers were within the confines of her underwear.

She sensed his arousal as she raised her hips before pounding down on him again. She hated to rush, but she couldn't control herself even if she wanted to; she was on the verge.

"In five, John!" Bill called out again.

"Yup, no problem. I'm coming," he replied.

Ella didn't even flinch this time. She was too engrossed in how John made her feel to care about anything else. She bounced with full force before succumbing.

"John … I'm—" Slamming her ass on top of him, her pussy contracted repeatedly. Multiple waves swept over her, leaving her dizzy from the frenzy of her movements.

John kissed all around her neck until her convulsions subsided. When Ella finally stopped shaking, he withdrew from inside her. She watched as he took his fingers, soaked in her juices, and rubbed them on his lips before sucking each one into his mouth. Ella felt butterflies in her stomach at the sight of such an intimate gesture.

"Damn, Ella, I thought you were going to cut off the circulation to them."

She was still breathing heavily when she dismounted him. "We can't have that. You need them to play."

"Yes, so true, and not just with my guitar."

She was sweating from exerting herself and from the sheer bliss of her climax.

"John, time!" It was Bill again.

She looked at John, and they both cracked up.

"You were wonderful, Ella. Will you stay for the show?"

She heard the longing in his voice. A part of her wanted to, but she wasn't sure. "You've got to go," she said.

He pulled her in for another kiss, a lengthy one that left her tingling.

"To be continued?" he said, combing his fingers through his hair.

His words sounded more like a statement than a question. She saw him walk out the door, patting down the creases of his shirt and tugging at his crotch to shake off his unfulfilled desire. She, however, smiled and was quite content to bask in the afterglow of her orgasm.

*   *   *   *

"I got your note. Not exactly what I was hoping for."

"Who …? What …? Who is this?" Ella was awakened out of a deep sleep. She'd almost dropped the cordless phone as she snatched it from its base. Consciousness crept in, and she peeked at the clock beside her bed. It was six thirty in the morning, on one of the few days she could normally sleep in.

"It's John. Remember me? The man you left last night with a raging hard-on?"

"How did you get my number?"

"I have my sources."

She was not in the phone book, but it wouldn't have been difficult for him to find her.

"It's early. Don't you sleep?" she asked.

"No, I couldn't stop thinking about you. I was looking forward to seeing you after the show."

"John, I'm sorry I left. I stayed for a few songs, but then—"

"But what? To say your note was brief is an understatement—'Thanks for a lovely time'? Is that all I was?"

Ella had known as she wrote it that he would be upset. She was aware the note was curt, but her intention had been to make a clean break.

"I had to go," she said.

"Obviously, you were in such a hurry you didn't even sign your name."

"John, please."

"What happened? I thought we had something."

They did, and Ella had felt it—that was the problem. Since reaching her midthirties, she had kept her younger men neatly compartmentalized. She picked them up, she determined when and where they fucked, and she ended it—usually after they had sex, which typically happened the same night she met them.

It was an unspoken rule—she was the older woman, and she called the shots. She never deluded herself into assuming something more could come out of a one-night stand. Things with John didn't quite happen that way, and she found him impossible to fit in a box.

"John, I don't normally—"

"What? Go out with guys my age?"

"No, that's not it."

"So, what's the problem then?"

"I—"

"Listen Ella, if you don't like me, tell me, but if you think there's an issue with my being younger than you, I can assure you there isn't."

"John, I'm thirty-eight, which makes me twelve years older than you."

"Fantastic."

"Fantastic?"

"Look, I don't give a damn how old you are. We connected and that's all I care about. You're a beautiful, sexy woman, and I want to see you again. Say you don't want the same thing, and I'll stop bothering you."

Ella sighed, and there was a moment of silence on the line. She remembered his skilled fingers on her.

The buzzer to her apartment went off. Who could that be on a Sunday morning?

"I like you, John. You're unlike anyone I've ever met."

"I'm glad to hear that, I'd hate to be a cliché."

The buzzer sounded again. Damn it, who was it at this hour?

Ella set the phone on speaker mode. She got out of bed and went to the bathroom to splash some cold water on her face. She was flushed from the conversation. Returning to her bedroom, she wrapped the bedsheet around her naked body.

"Am I beginning to wear you down?" he asked.

"Perhaps," she said as she walked through the living room.

"Good."

Now there was a knock on the door.

"Shit," she muttered. "John, there's someone at my door. Let me go see who it is."

She went to open it.

"Hello, Ella," he said.

She saw John standing there, his hair a mess, cell phone in hand, and looking more delicious than she remembered.

*   *   *   *

After her initial shock of seeing him, she let him in.

"You don't waste any time, do you?" she said.

Shedding his jacket, he stood facing her in the living room. "I didn't get a chance to finish what we started."

"You are resourceful. I'll give you that."

"I know what I want."

"I see." She felt flushed all over. "How did you get in the building?"

"A nice old lady let me in. I think she was leaving for church."

"Security just isn't what it used to be."

"When I said I couldn't stop thinking of you, Ella—I meant it. The taste of you kept me awake all night."

Ella breathed deeply and recalled the way he'd smeared her cum on his lips. "I hope it didn't affect your performance."

"It improved it."

She gave him a weak smile. It was small talk, and they both knew it.

The way he was leering at her made her blush. She felt almost paralyzed, but then she let the sheet cascade off her to form a puddle around her ankles.

"Fuck …," he said.

He walked over and grabbed her, forcibly drawing her to him in one hard move. With one hand, he brushed the hair away from her face; with the other, he clutched her ass, pulling her even closer to him. He planted his mouth on hers with such ferocity that it made Ella feel faint. She opened up, sucking on him while she grappled with his jeans, unzipping them and trying to get them off him. He helped her, shed his underwear as well, and then kicked them clear across the room. With one quick motion, he whipped off his T-shirt, and they fell on the couch together. Ella sat on top of him, kissing him, her tongue tickling his palate.

John seized her boobs, and she bent backward. He took her large and sensitive nipples between his lips, alternating licks between each one. Ella had always considered her small plum-shaped breasts to be one of her best features.

His fingertips were calloused, likely from playing the guitar, and his hands were chafed but not rough. When he fondled her, she felt the power behind the music he created and loved being his instrument.

"Ella, you've made me crazy. I had a boner all night thinking about you."

She guessed he hadn't slept, given his pent-up frustration. Now he was fighting to keep from losing control—and it was time to exert hers.

Ella held his head, which he'd deposited in her bosom and guided his lips to hers. She wanted to slow things down. She explored the curves and ridges of his mouth. She still smelled herself on him, and it turned her on even more. When she advanced to bite his neck and ears, she felt him poke her in the belly. She got off the couch and knelt in front of him on the floor.

"I think I need to take care of you," she said. "You've waited long enough."

He gazed at her, not saying a word. His breathing was shallow. She knew he was mesmerized by the thought of what she was about to do to him.

She took a pillow to kneel on and gasped when she saw his young, stiff cock. John's penis was a remarkable sight. It was perfectly straight, and the tip was already moist with frustration. He was big, probably seven inches long, but what really got her attention was how thick he was. She closed her eyes for a moment to imagine how he would feel inside her.

"See what I mean?" he said. "I haven't been able to get him down all night."

"We'll have to fix that, won't we?"

Ella tasted the wet bead that had formed over his glans. She inhaled the musky aroma before darting her tongue around the knob.

She felt John's fingers in her hair and looked up to see him watching her. She could tell he was in ecstasy. Ella heard him groan as she licked the underside of his cock. With one hand, she reached up to touch his chest. He was firm with very little hair. She tweaked his nipples and felt them stand up erect before running her nails along his washboard abdomen.

Ella continued nibbling John until she sensed he was ready to explode, but before she took him inside her, she burrowed between his legs to become acquainted with his testicles.

John was squirming now, pushing himself toward her. She knew he wanted her to devour him. Gripping him at the base, she encircled her lips over his bulbous head. Holding him tightly, she glided her palm along his shaft as she sucked him in. She proceeded with her unhurried blow job, bobbing until she sensed tiny tremors arising from within him. Concurrently, she ran her tongue across the rim in a continuous spiral.

Ella took him deeper into her throat. She relaxed her muscles so she was able to swallow repeatedly, creating vibrations against him with her vocal chords and her lips. It was not long before she felt spasms course through him.

He let go of her hair and flung his arms atop the back of the couch. Ella saw he was preparing to surrender. She grabbed his ass and dug her nails into his fleshy cheeks. He tensed, and convulsions surged through him.

"Oh ... fuck!" he said, spurting his cum in several erratic thrusts.

She tried gulping as much as she could, but it was impossible. His cream spilled out the corners of her mouth and dribbled down her chin—she didn't stop sucking him.

John came for some time, and she massaged his balls until he was completely emptied. His erection did not die immediately. Ella now realized he was not kidding when he said he had saved it up—he certainly had an abundance to give her.

"Oh, my god ... Ella."

She climbed on top of him again and kissed him. In the light of day, she realized how intense the blue of his eyes was. It was not a baby blue, as she had first thought, but a rich violet color. In them, she saw the spirit of an old soul.

"Did you like that?" she asked.

"Are you joking with me?" He was out of breath. "I've never had a blow job like that."

"As a musician, I thought you'd appreciate a hummer."

"It was fantastic. I hope I wasn't too much for you."

"I admit you probably exceeded my daily requirement of protein!" She wiped her chin with her fingers and touched them to her nipples.

He seemed slightly self-conscious. "Ella ..."

She was enjoying how he looked at her as she spread his semen around her breasts. "No worries, John. You weren't too much." She grinned. "In fact, you were just perfect."

*   *   *   *

They took a shower together, and it was John's turn to see Ella more closely now.

"I knew you were shaven when I touched you last night. I've never seen that before." He was referring to her "landing strip." Ella preferred to go hairless otherwise, and she got a Brazilian wax every six weeks.

John recovered quickly after their shower and tried to initiate another make-out session, but Ella restrained herself. She couldn't deny how turned on he made her feel, but it was uncharted territory for her. She needed time to think about what she wanted to do.

It was a crisp autumn morning as they walked out of her place in the Lower East Side. For the past few weeks, cooler days had replaced the humidity of the hot city. Ella loved the dog days of summer, but she had to admit the fall was a welcome change, given she didn't own an air-conditioner.

They were seated at her favorite greasy spoon, just up the corner from her apartment. They both ordered steak and eggs and settled in for a leisurely breakfast.

"So how did you get to be part owner of Madame Z?" she asked.

John had a sip of his coffee. "My father bought it about five years ago with my older brother, James. Dad always dreamt of owning a blues club."

"Was he in the business?"

"No, he was just a real music fan. I got my love of jazz and blues from him."

"And your brother—he was into music too?"

"Yes, but in a different way. He liked the lifestyle—he enjoyed being with musicians."

"How long have you been playing guitar?"

"Since I was about seven, my dad encouraged me to take up an instrument, and one day he put on John Lee Hooker's 'Boogie Chillun'.' After that, I was hooked, no pun intended."

"You were named after him, weren't you?"

"Yes, he was one of Dad's favorites."

"Isn't it funny that we were both named after musicians?"

"Yes, great names, both of them—but difficult to live up to."

"For me, definitely. I know so little about jazz, and can't sing to save my life, but you play like your namesake."

"Thanks, but I still have a lot to learn."

Ella liked his modesty, even though she had heard part of his performance and thought he sounded sensational.

"It must have taken a lot of hard work."

"Yeah, when other kids were riding their bikes or shooting hoops, I was home practicing blues riffs."

"You seem very disciplined."

He paused a moment, and she sensed there was something he wanted to tell her.

"I don't know about that. I gave up blues for a while."

"It's only natural to try different things when you're young."

"Of course, but I knew I would come back to it eventually. I just wasn't prepared for how it happened."

"What do you mean?" She was fascinated.

The server brought their orders, and amid a flurry of condiments, cutting of food, and more coffee, John continued.

"My parents died a few years ago, a freak accident on the highway."

"That's awful. I'm sorry, John."

"Yeah, it was a rough period." He stared off into the distance, and Ella gave him a moment.

"So it's just the two of you?"

"Yeah, just me and James."

"And you took your father's place when he passed away?"

"Actually, no, my uncle did, and then he removed James as partner and asked me to join him instead."

Ella was missing something. "Your brother didn't want to do it anymore?"

"He wasn't able to. He was a drug addict and had been in and out of rehab. My parents were going to visit him in a hospital in Syracuse when they had the accident."

"How tragic." Ella couldn't imagine what John had endured at such an early age.

"Yes, it was brutal. James blamed himself, and he was in no condition to run a club. My uncle's a lawyer and was executor of my parents' estate, so he looked after the finances, but he didn't know anything about music."

"So it was a natural fit for you."

"In a way, though it took me awhile to find my place there."

"Of course. It couldn't have been easy to step into your brother's shoes."

"Oh, no, it wasn't that. James never ran the place. My dad made him a partner to give him something to belong to. Unfortunately, it didn't work out."

"I see. Were you angry he didn't offer you a partnership to begin with?"

"No, not at all. I was too young then. I was also in a band, so I had my own thing going on."

"Are you and your brother in touch?"

"Yes, every few weeks. He's been clean since our parents died. I think their deaths scared him straight, or maybe the guilt did."

"He doesn't want to return to the business?"

"No, he has no interest, says I'm better at handling the scene, whatever that means."

Ella noticed how John took a mouthful of food and chewed nervously while trying to dismiss his brother's comment. "I think it's pretty clear what he means."

"Really?"

"Yes, he's knows you're the one who will fulfill your dad's vision for the club."

John stopped eating and frowned. He looked at Ella, and she could see he was in deep thought. Had she said something to offend him? Though it was certainly not her intention, Ella knew she was often too outspoken, and her words could sometimes be construed as tactless.

He leaned forward and kissed her slowly, licking her lips, and she tasted the ketchup on his tongue. She was both confused and relieved by his reaction.

"You're very perceptive, Ella."

"I'm sorry. I hope I didn't say anything to upset you."

"No, it's just that—"

"You don't have to explain—"

"No, I want to. My father had great plans for the club. When he first bought it, I wasn't all that interested because I was touring, and it wasn't with a blues band."

"What was it?"

"Rockabilly, mostly."

"Funny, I don't picture you playing that."

"No, I liked it, but it's not what was in my soul, and I wanted to get back to the blues anyway."

"And now you have."

"True. Although I wish my dad were still around to see me perform at the club. I know he's gone, but I'll always consider it *his* club."

"I'm sure he's listening from wherever he is."

"Yeah, I hope so."

She saw sadness in his eyes, but there was something else there too. "Are you all right?" she asked.

"It'll be exactly three years ago tomorrow since my parents died. I haven't talked about this in a long time."

"Is there anything I can do?" Ella had a sudden urge to reach out and hug him.

"Yes, actually."

"What is it?"

"Have dinner with me tomorrow night, my place. I'll cook."

She had wanted to take it slow. "John, are you sure? Wouldn't you rather spend it with someone you feel closer to?"

"I feel close to you."

She found it impossible to say no to him.

*   *   *   *

John lived in Greenwich Village—the opposite side of the city from Ella. When she arrived at his address, she discovered that it was a beautiful loft, complete with doorman service.

"Nice place you have here," she said, walking in and casually handing him a bottle of wine when he opened the door.

"Thanks."

Nervous, she had thought about calling him as late as a few hours before their date to cancel it. In the end, she knew the only reason she was apprehensive was because she had let him control the situation. She just needed to remember that it would not lead to anything, even though she liked him very much.

Ella surveyed the high-beamed ceilings and wood floors. She saw that there were at least two bedrooms, and the kitchen looked newly renovated. There was music playing softly in the background.

John came up from behind her and touched her shoulder. She turned to him.

"I forgot to do something when you first came in."

"What's that?" she asked.

He kissed her. It was long and deep, and it left her wanting. She dissolved into him and felt her stomach flutter as he held her in his arms.

"Welcome to my home, Ella."

"Thank you. Is it hot in here … or is it just me?"

"We're the ones heating up the place," he said.

They snickered at how corny they sounded.

"I think that could be the start of a blues song, don't you?" she asked.

"No, I'd say those are more like country lyrics."

"True!" she said, knowing how bad some of those lyrics could be.

John looked great wearing black jeans and a gray T-shirt. It was a cool evening, and Ella had spent almost half an hour deciding what to wear. She finally threw on a sleeveless wool dress, draped with a pashmina scarf. It was unlike her to fuss so much for a date, but then again, she couldn't remember the last time she'd had one. According to her girlfriends, she didn't have dates—she had "fuck sessions."

"Can I help you with anything?" The place smelled terrific, and she wasn't sure what he was making for dinner.

"No, it's almost done. Why don't you take care of the wine?" he said.

Ella sat on one of the stools at the kitchen island and watched him make last-minute touches.

"What are we having?"

"Take a guess."

"We already know I'm a bad guesser, remember?"

He chuckled. "Okay, I'll give you a hint, and you only have to come up with the *type* of food we're having."

"That should be easier … I think."

"It's a night to celebrate the blues."

"Okay." She pulled the cork out of the bottle.

"So I cooked in the tradition of African Americans responsible for blues music."

"Hmm." She noticed he was cutting a leafy green vegetable. "Would that be soul food?"

"Correct! See, you're not so bad after all."

"Yay! Do I win anything?"

He stopped chopping and walked over to her.

"What would you like?" he asked.

She blushed, so easily seduced by him.

John moved in to kiss her, and she sensed a shower of heat in her loins rising up to her cheeks. She had never felt this way before with a man, and at times, she had to remind herself he was only twenty-six. Ella poured the wine, and he proposed a toast.

"To my dad, for nurturing my love of music, and to my parents—gone but not forgotten."

They clinked glasses and had a sip of the Napa Valley Cabernet Ella had brought.

"Beautiful toast, John. Your parents would have been proud. I can't imagine what it's like to lose them both like that."

"Shitty. They had a wonderful marriage, and there was so much more they wanted to do. You just never think …" He stared at his glass absentmindedly and swirled it against the counter.

There was silence, but it was not uncomfortable. When he looked up at her again, she kissed him—a slow, lingering caress of her lips on his—until she felt a stirring in her stomach.

"What was that for?" he asked.

"No reason. Just happy to be here."

"I'm happy you're here too—I really didn't want to be alone tonight."

It was Ella's first glimpse of John's vulnerable side.

*   *   *   *

"Have you been to any soul food places up in Harlem?" he asked.

"Just to Aunt Ruth's Restaurant. I liked it."

"You should. It's one of the best in town, and where I got some of these recipes."

They were enjoying a meal of ribs, candied yams, and collard greens. Ella took another piece of corn bread.

"This is the best corn bread I've ever had. I can't believe you made this."

"That was the most difficult part of the entire meal."

"It's fantastic. I love the jalapenos in it. It's got a bite."

"You can really eat, but it doesn't show on you."

"I have a healthy appetite."

"Good to know. There're plenty of ribs left."

"Thanks. They're great." She was messy and had accumulated a huge pile of bones on her plate and sticky barbecue sauce all over her fingers. There was something raw and sensual about eating with her hands. Between the wine and the spicy bread, she was feeling both hot and flustered.

"Who's playing right now?" Ella asked.

John listened a second. "This is Albert King. Do you like it?"

"Yes. 'Born Under a Bad Sign.' I know this song, but not by him."

"He originally recorded it back in sixty-seven, but it's been covered by other artists."

"You're right. It was done by Cream."

"Clapton's band," he said.

"So you do know a little about rock music."

"I know him because he's a guitarist. Most of his influences stem from the blues."

"I see. I didn't realize blues had such a big impact on rock music."

"It certainly does, more than people would think. Many rock icons owe their careers to blues artists."

"Like who?"

"Like Elvis, the Stones, Van Morrison—"

"Van the Man?"

"Oh, yes, absolutely."

"He's one of my favorites, reinventing himself constantly—a very resilient artist."

"True, his main influences were Muddy Waters and Charlie Parker. He and John Lee Hooker were also friends."

"Right, they had quite a few collaborations."

"Didn't they put out an album together? It was called—"

"*Don't Look Back*," she said.

"That's the one."

Ella was impressed to be having a conversation with this man about music they both listened to and liked.

"You know a lot about music, but I'll bet you don't know a little known fact about Van Morrison that *I* know," she said.

"Oh?"

"Yes." She motioned him to come closer, as if she had a secret to share.

He leaned in, his face just inches from hers.

"Have you heard his song 'Brown Eyed Girl'?" she asked.

"Yes." John appeared genuinely intrigued.

She turned to whisper in his ear. "He wrote that for me."

"Really?" He looked at her, feigning surprise.

Ella grinned and nodded, feeling lightheaded from the wine. "Yes, and don't believe any stories to the contrary."

"Ella."

"Yes?"

"I'm crazy about you."

"Oh." She couldn't say anything else. She had wanted to be funny, but she was also aware that she was flirting with him, and it felt good. She knew he was smitten with her, but was that what she truly wanted?

*   *   *   *

John had picked up sweet potato pie for dessert. It was the only part of dinner he didn't make, but Ella was too full. They decided to take a break from the meal.

"Come, I want to show you something," he said.

"Okay, where are we going?"

"My studio."

She followed him into a room she'd initially thought was a second bedroom. Filled with at least ten guitars, amplifiers, and recording equipment, there was also a computer and a couple of flat-screen monitors on a desk. It was a decent size and felt cool and airy. On the walls hung large posters of legendary musicians, most of them in black and white.

"What a great room," she said. "Is this where you create your music?"

"Yes, and it's a place to store my guitars."

"Do you write your own stuff?"

"For a while now. I'm trying to put it all together."

"Excellent. You should record an album."

"That's the plan."

"I'd buy it."

"I'll hold you to that," he said.

Ella walked around the room. "Fantastic posters." She recognized the ones of John Lee Hooker and Robert Johnson, but there were a few she didn't know. She was staring at one of an older black woman.

"That's Ma Rainey," John said. "She's considered 'Mother of the Blues.'"

"And who's that?" Ella stood in front of another female—only she was much younger.

"Sister Rosetta Tharpe—she mastered the guitar by the age of six. She started as a gospel singer but then changed over to blues in the fifties—hell of a performer. If you get a chance, look at some old footage of her singing 'Down by the Riverside.' She's riveting."

"I will, and that's a beautiful instrument she's holding too."

"Yes, a Gibson SG—standard for blues."

"Is that what you have?"

"No, mine is a Gibson ES 335. It's one John Lee Hooker also played." He took it off the rack to show her—it had a rich cherry finish.

Ella ran her hand across the neck of it. "That is one gorgeous instrument."

"It sure is."

"Will you perform something for me?"

"You mean ... now? Here?"

"Yes."

He appeared reticent. "I don't know ..."

"Oh, come on. Don't tell me no one has ever asked you to do that ..."

"Actually, no. No one has."

It surprised her that he seemed so reserved. "You mean to say you've never played for any of your girlfriends here before?" Ella was fishing, though she was trying not to be too obvious.

"No, I don't bring anyone in this room, but I'll do it for you … if that's what you want."

She almost felt sorry for being so presumptuous. Thankfully, he didn't seem put off by her comments. "Yes, I'd very much like to hear you play."

"Any special requests?" he asked.

"No, but a blues song would be good." Ella sat on a nearby chair.

John brought out a different guitar and plugged it into an amplifier.

"That's a Dobro, isn't it?" she asked.

"That's right. You're familiar with it?"

"Yes, the first time I heard one live was at a Mark Knopfler concert."

"Former lead man for Dire Straits—excellent guitarist."

"It's a unique sound."

"Well, I hope you enjoy this, then."

She loved the way he looked setting up his instrument. She guessed that the metal Dobro must have been quite heavy, as his muscles flexed in his arms when he held it. He also attached a harmonica to the neck brace he placed around himself.

"You look just like Dylan!" she said, howling with delight.

"I sure hope I look better than him!"

"Of course."

She thought rock musicians were hot when they performed on stage, but having a private show in John's studio was so much sexier.

"All right. Here's a song from one of my favorites," he said. "Have you heard of Taj Mahal?"

"I'm assuming we're not referring to the mausoleum in India."

"No, we're not."

"I didn't think so."

He shook his head, and Ella could tell he was amused.

"Taj Mahal was born Henry St. Claire Fredericks, here in Harlem. His mother sang in a gospel choir, and his father was a jazz pianist."

"So he was brought up with music."

"Yes, unfortunately, his father had to work on a farm to support the family. He was later killed when a tractor fell on him."

"How terrible."

"It sure was. Taj Mahal was barely a teen at the time. Later, a neighbor taught him the guitar, and he's been at it ever since. It's been more than forty years, and he still tours today."

"Fabulous, now that's staying power."

"That's what I admire about him. Like your man, Van Morrison, Taj Mahal constantly reinvents himself. He's also one of the few blues Dobro players."

Ella loved that John talked about music with so much authority and enthusiasm.

"I'll do a song from his album *Phantom Blues*. Clapton and Bonnie Raitt also appeared on it."

"Sounds good. What's it called?"

"The name of the song is 'Lovin' in my Baby's Eyes.'"

Ella sat with her elbows on her knees, and rested her chin in her hands. She listened intently and saw how John fluidly moved his fingers across the guitar as he sucked and blew the harp. The raw quality of his voice was captivating.

It was a song with simple lyrics, but they resonated deeply with her. They spoke about how he wanted to be her man, and how he would do anything in the world for her to see the love in her eyes.

If machinery could weep, its cries would be the sounds John made with his Dobro. As she watched the pained expressions on his face, she was moved beyond anything she had ever experienced. The way he looked at her when he sang the words made her believe the lyrics had been written just for her.

Ella clapped when he finished. The song had made her hot—really hot. She wanted him, but she felt glued to her seat. It was as if she were thinking inappropriate thoughts in John's sacred space. She was completely mesmerized by the song and could not remember when she was more touched by something a man did for her.

"How was that?" he asked.

"I loved it, everything about it."

He returned the guitar to the stand, turned off the amplifier, and walked over to her.

"I've done that song so many times with no one in mind, but now …"

"John, I—"

"No, let me finish Ella. It's corny as hell, but it's the love in *your* eyes I want to see."

"John—"

"I know you have reservations about me because of my age, but—"

"John! Please let me say something." She stood up and couldn't hold back any longer.

"Sorry, go ahead."

"Do you know how I feel right now?"

"I'm afraid to ask."

"Ask."

"All right, how do you feel?"

"More turned on than I've ever felt in my entire life."

*   *   *   *

The sexual tension between them was excruciating, so much so that when John's lips brushed hers, she melted into his arms and was barely able to stand. He swung her off her feet into his arms and carried her to his bedroom. She buried her head in the nape of his neck and kissed him. She wanted him so badly it hurt. She had never had anyone perform for her, nor had she ever been so seduced by a song.

His bedroom was located down the hall from his studio. Its sparse furnishings included a king-size bed, a couple of night tables, and a pair of in-wall speakers.

He laid her on the bed and switched on a lamp. The room was painted a rich dark chocolate color. It was masculine but still warm. John lit a couple of small candles and turned off the light.

Ella shook with anticipation. She realized she had given up control, and to her amazement, she actually liked it. She reasoned that it was probably something she had always wanted to do but had never met the right man to surrender to.

John had maturity, passion, and intelligence—qualities she thought were impossible to find in someone his age. She was wrong.

He stood by the bed, ogling her as she lay breathless with need for him. He started unbuckling his belt. He took his time undressing. When he finally stood naked in front of her, Ella got up on her knees.

She knelt on the bed and held her arms above her head as John pulled off her dress. His erection pointed directly at her. Wearing only her bra and panties, she reached for his cock and held it in her hand. She heard him sigh.

"You can't know how aroused I was by your performance."

"Show me," he said.

She curled her lips around his knob, drawing him down her gullet. Gripping his shaft, she slid out slowly, and then she took him in again. Ella felt him get harder with each stroke.

While in her mouth, she tongued him, feeling the ridges and veins along the full length of him. She was a wild woman, intent on consuming his dick, until she sensed his fingers interlaced in her hair, stopping her. She tried pulling him in by grabbing his buttocks—desperate to have him inside her.

"No, Ella ... no." He seemed ready to explode but nowhere near ready to stop. He got on the bed and covered her body with his, kissing her lips so violently they were certain to become bruised. Ella felt an incredible amount of heat building up in her. Just when she couldn't take it anymore, John nipped to the area below her collarbone and remained there, biting her flushed skin.

She was panting, her chest rising and falling as he stared at her. She saw the lust in his eyes as he easily unfastened her front clasp bra. He teased her breasts until she arched her back to beg for more.

"Tell me, Ella, tell me what you want."

"I want ... I want you to play me the way you play your music."

"Hmm ... I can do that. I'll pretend you're my favorite guitar."

He hovered over her, and she could hardly wait for his touch. He tasted her peaks, savoring each one. He bit around them and then flicked them with the rigid tip of his tongue until they both stood erect. At the same time, he pushed her mounds together to kiss deep in her cleavage.

John moved lower with his lips but continued to play with her nipples. One moment, it felt like he was finger picking a tune at a fast tempo; the next, he slowed it right down as if he were bending a guitar string, changing the pitch to elicit a different sound from her.

Ella was aware of the stickiness that had formed between her legs. She was almost afraid he would have to peel off her underwear, knowing she had already soaked through them while in his studio.

"John, please ..."

Within seconds, he had removed her panties. He held them to his nose and breathed her in. "Ella, your scent drives me insane."

She thought she would go crazy if he didn't touch her that second. He placed her calves on top of his shoulders and spread her labia to fondle her. He slathered her juices all around her pussy and massaged it into her hot box.

She gasped and sunk into the pillow. She didn't have the strength to watch as he ravaged her. She was the instrument, and he was the virtuoso. John removed his fingers from her and replaced them with his tongue, spearing her with carnal brutality. She swore she almost lost consciousness.

John gave her mean, mean licks, clutching her ass to gorge himself on her. He wagged in and out, sucked her like a harmonica, and released her. When she writhed for more, he stabbed her again. Back and forth, he played with her, lightly tickling the entrance to her hole and drinking her in.

Ella's moans escalated, emanating from within her diaphragm. John fluttered to her clit and enclosed his mouth on top of it, vibrating her nub. She heard him feasting on her like a wild beast and could no longer contain herself.

She convulsed and gushed cum all over John's face. She was swept up by one rapturous wave after another. John drank in her sweetness and waited. She continued to whimper, more wetness leaking from her. He lingered there—breathing softly, moving slowly, like strumming a ballad. Soon her tempo changed, and she knew she was not yet finished.

He placed his palm on her mound and applied gentle pressure—it was all she could take. From somewhere far up her snatch, Ella felt a second eruption gain speed. It wrenched through her groin, zigzagged across her breasts to her throat, and finally had her singing the blues.

"Ohhh …" Her voice was not her own, and she was astonished by the sound of it.

John lay with his mouth on her pussy and lapped her up. He was glazed with her honey, and when he ascended her body with kisses, she sucked his lips and indulged in the essence of her own sex.

"You're incredible, Ella."

She heard the desire in his voice and knew he ached for her; that much was clear. He reached into the drawer and took out a condom, tearing it open with his teeth. It was agonizing for her to wait the few seconds before she had him inside her.

"John, I can't wait. I—"

Neither could he. Before she could say another word, he plunged into her with such ferocity that he made her head spin. Her pussy clenched his shaft like a fist. He moved slowly at first, but she knew that couldn't last. She wrapped her arms and legs around him, urging him into her warm chamber. Ella's frenzy spurred him on faster and faster. His cock felt like fire inside her. Never before had she been so possessed by a man.

She felt every inch of him as he jabbed into her. When he slid out, he poked her sensitive entrance, nestling there for less than a second before he dove into her again. He changed up the pace by circling his hips, which enabled her to savor the thickness of him.

He continued to fuck her savagely. She bit down on her lower lip when she felt herself peaking again and dug her nails into his back. Pulsations radiated throughout her being.

Ella came with full force, drenching her twat, squeezing John's prick as the swells attacked every nerve in her body. She thrashed and convulsed until she overflowed, soaking the sheets with her sticky fluid.

John was on his knees now. He swung her legs on top of his shoulders and plummeted into her.

"Fuck!" he yelled.

He was twitching uncontrollably, but he didn't stop swiveling his hips. Ella could feel how deeply planted he was in her, and he was only getting harder. She was shocked—he was not yet finished.

"Ella, I can't get enough of you."

"My god, John …" she said. She didn't want to stop either.

She placed a pillow behind her and hugged her knees up to her chest. John advanced closer and penetrated her even deeper.

He drilled in slowly, leaning in to lick her breasts and nipples. He kissed her lips and sucked on them with unbridled lust. He was so rooted in her cavern that she felt him rubbing up against her G-spot.

"Oh, John …"

She loved saying his name as he glided inside her like playing a red-hot slide guitar. He teased her and she cried out, which only prompted him to fuck her wildly. Every stroke increased the pressure building up in her loins.

Ella wasn't sure she could come again without passing out, but she desperately wanted to. She also didn't know how it was possible, but it felt like he was growing bigger inside her. She reached behind him to hold on to his firm cheeks.

He was really going at it now and was wet from her fluids and his sweat. She shut her eyes and swore she heard a spark ignite from within her abdomen. Ella was delirious from the roar of another climax. Each spasm was stronger than the previous one, making it difficult for her to catch her breath. She cried out as she came, letting out a lengthy wail while she dug her nails into John's ass and inserted a finger in his anus.

He held her tightly as she gyrated through her orgasm. When she stopped quivering, he growled incoherently into her ear just before his thrusts became staccato.

"Ella!" he grunted as he slammed into her, invading her with a hot surge. He jerked repeatedly from the explosion. She saw him finally succumb to his convulsions before collapsing on top of her.

*   *   *   *

"El-laaa … Oh, El-laaa," he whispered in her ear, chewing lightly on her lobe.

"What?"

"Ella, my sexy Ella."

"Huh? What time is it?" she asked, waking up from a sound sleep.

"It's almost eight."

"How long have you been up?"

"Since seven."

"You don't like to sleep, do you?"

"I usually get up with the sunrise, and now with fall here, I'm getting more than enough sleep. You asked me to wake you up early this morning."

"I did?" Ella was still groggy, and it took her a few seconds to realize where she was.

"Yup, though you were on the verge of falling asleep when you said it."

Ella was confused, not recalling asking him that. She rubbed the sleep from her eyes and tried to remember all the things he'd done to her. Her body felt completely ravaged, and slowly but surely, permeating her thoughts were the multiple orgasms she had experienced. She shivered—no wonder she couldn't think straight.

She lay under the bedsheet, but he was beside her on top of it—naked and semi-hard. A flood of heat enveloped her as she glanced at him. She tried not to focus on his naked body. Suddenly, it hit her what day it was.

"My god, now I know why I asked you to wake me up. I have an early meeting. It is Tuesday, isn't it?"

"Yes … it's Tuesday, and you know what else, Ella?"

"What?"

"You're delightful."

She sensed real affection from him, something she wasn't used to. He had broken down her walls to where she felt safe to relinquish control—it was a wonderful feeling to let go. Ella tried to get up, but John draped a heavy arm and leg over her so she couldn't move.

"Hey!" She protested, laughing and falling back on the bed.

"You're not going anywhere—not yet. Not till I get one thing straight."

Ella rolled on her stomach, and turned to face him.

He lay on his side with his head in his palm, propped up by his elbow.

"Okay," she said, feeling slightly anxious. "What is it?"

"You know that Van Morrison song?"

"Which one?"

"The one you said he wrote for you."

She snickered in amusement. "You mean 'Brown Eyed Girl'?"

"That's the one."

"What about it?"

"I'd like to bet he didn't write it for you."

"Really? And how do you intend to prove it?"

"Easy. Just answer this one question for me."

"Okay."

"Has he ever gotten close enough to see your brown eyes?"

He had her there. "No, I can't say he has."

"Well, I have, and I see something really special in them."

Ella extended her hand to touch his cheek. "What do you see?"

"I see you in my life."

"Is that so?" She felt so taken with this young man. "And what else?"

"Like all great music, I see us with staying power."

Ella leaned in and kissed him. He had charmed her in a way no man ever had. Though their age difference still concerned her, she was at least willing to give their relationship a chance. As for staying power—only time would tell. If last night's performance was any indication of John's endurance, she was optimistic they could be making music together for a long time.

act three

Stella Christy had been divorced two years before she met Norman, and that was after ending a conservative decade-long marriage. Her husband had been a traditionalist. Sex was silent, missionary style, and utterly unfulfilling for her. She didn't know she had diverse needs until her midthirties, and her husband was unwilling to indulge any of them. With no children to tie them together, she could no longer stay with him.

Stella was thirty-eight, a petite five feet four, but she could easily pass for thirty—something she attributed to being a vegetarian and yoga classes at least three times a week. She turned heads because of her severe appearance, which she put a lot of effort into maintaining. Someone once likened her to a dangerous black panther. Her hair was naturally blond, but she dyed it blue-black and wore it in a pageboy-bob style. Oversized emerald green eyes offset her pale complexion and accentuated full, luscious lips that looked like they could suck the life out of a man. The rest of her was average but very well put together. She oozed sexuality.

Stella and Norman had been seeing each other for a little over a year, having met through an adult chat line for sexually curious people. After six months, she had learned exactly what he liked and was willing to indulge him as no one else would. That made her irresistible to him. Now she wanted to enact one of her own fantasies.

"You know what I would love to have?" she asked.

"What?"

"A ménage à trois."

Norman gawked at her. "You're kidding."

"No, I'm not. Wouldn't you?"

"No … Actually, I never thought of it."

They were about to turn in, and it was all part of her master plan to bring it up at that moment. She continued staring at herself in the dresser mirror, brushing her hair. It was her ritual—one hundred strokes every night. She saw Norman sitting up in bed behind her and tried to sound casual.

"Yes, and it would be us with another man."

"No fucking way!" he shouted. "A woman, maybe—and that's a *big* maybe—but another man, not a chance."

"Why not?" She kept her voice calm, silently counting the number of brush strokes—seventy-nine, eighty, eighty-one …

"Stella, I've only just gotten used to you, and I don't want to introduce new people into our games."

"Yes, but what if I find someone who takes good direction?"

"Are you deliberately trying to piss me off?"

"No, Norman, we're just having a conversation here." She'd known that bringing this up would rile him.

"A conversation? You're trying to provoke me again, aren't you?"

"How do you mean?" she said, acting coy, continuing the count—ninety, ninety-one, ninety-two …

"The last time we had a conversation like this, I ended up indulging one of your other crazy whims. You remember, the one with that friend of yours—that animal—Jake."

Jake was an old chum of hers from college. She found out he was gay when they reconnected following her divorce. He was the sweetest man, but his appearance was intimidating if you didn't know him. One evening, he confessed he wanted to seduce a straight man.

"You're exaggerating, Norman. Jake's not an animal."

"The man's six and a half feet tall, bald, and weighs three hundred pounds. What would you call him?"

She laughed. "You had fun though, didn't you?"

He paused, but he didn't refute her. Jake ended up giving Norman a blow job, probably better than any he had ever received from a woman, including herself. She knew he had enjoyed it, but there was no way he would ever admit it.

"Stella," Norman said. "Why are you bringing up the threesome thing? Don't I please you?"

She replaced the brush in the dresser drawer and turned to look at him with affection. "My darling Norman, of course you please me. I was just hoping for a bit of variety. That's the name of the game, isn't it?"

"I just don't want to lose my queen."

Stella detected a slight hint of jealousy in his voice, but when he called her that, it was his cue that he wanted to play. "I'll always be your queen, I promise. Perhaps my king is thirsty and desires a drink from my love fountain."

"You dirty vixen, come here," he said.

She sauntered over to him and kissed his Roman nose. She could seduce Norman into almost anything as long as he was able to dive into her shaven muff.

"My king, I have been very bad. I need you to punish me with your hard whip of a tongue."

"Yes, my queen, you have had bad thoughts, and I must teach you a lesson. It's for your own good."

He lay on the bed, naked and already aroused. She removed her satin negligee and stood above him facing the headboard, legs on either side of his face. She squatted and hovered her pussy just over his chin.

"King Norman, please show me the error of my ways."

Norman's wet tickler darted out and jabbed her hot hole. She held on to the bed for support and sat lower. She felt his fingers touch her, probe her, spread her labia wide open.

"Queen Stella, you will be punished. I will feel you remorseful with your juices raining down on me."

"Yes, Your Highness."

He assailed her, flicking her clit, licking her viciously. She did a slow gyration to ensure he didn't miss any part of her and started to moan.

"Quiet!" He abruptly pushed her off him. "I'm punishing you. It's not meant for you to enjoy yourself!" he shouted.

"Yes, my king …" Stella was in heaven. "My apologies."

He resumed eating her with abandon and smeared her honey back and forth along her slit. He chewed her lips, making them puffier than they already were—he penetrated her with a finger, then a second one.

"Please, my king, please …"

"Please what?"

"Please don't go easy on me. I have been very bad, very bad indeed."

"Queen Stella, I will have no mercy upon you. Rest assured of that."

She was really moving her hips now and felt his stiff tip nudge her clit repeatedly. He took great liberties to explore her, and she was beginning to feel dizzy. She loved this position. He was below her, yet *she* was the one being punished—it was the paradox of the fantasy. Norman's twisted idea of discipline was to perform oral sex on her. What woman wouldn't want that? After a lifetime of not having it, she couldn't get enough.

She was close to coming and kept circling her hips. His beard scratched her like a scouring pad in the most seductive way—in her crack, on her sensitive bud, and against her skin.

"My king, I have seen the error of my ways."

"Alas, I don't trust you have."

"Oh …" She felt herself peaking and knew she wouldn't be able hold back much longer.

"You control yourself, Queen Stella. You don't come until I say you can. You hear me?"

"No, please …" She was panting now. "Don't punish me like this. I'll be better … I promise."

He pulled her on top of him until she sat directly on his mouth. He stuck his tongue farther inside her. Taking his middle finger, sufficiently lubricated from her secretions and his saliva, he inserted it into her anus.

"Oh, oh …" Her muscles flexed around him.

Norman released her to issue a warning. "Hold it, Queen Stella," he said. "Don't you dare, not until I say so."

Stella was almost delirious as he continued his assault, sliding his finger higher up her tight little asshole. She had never been eaten better by anyone in her life. Norman loved oral sex, and he knew exactly how she liked it.

"My king, please …"

He tortured her clit. Her legs were wobbly.

"Do you promise to be good?"

"Yes … yes …"

"Do you promise not to annoy your king?"

"Yes, I promise …"

"Do you promise not to bring up the threesome again?"

She could only think of her desire. "Yes … I promise." She started to convulse.

"All right, my queen, you may shower me with your sweet nectar."

Stella, a huge comer, splashed Norman several times. He lapped her up, drank in her honey, and sucked her so she could get another orgasm out of it—she did.

"My king!" she cried when she drenched him again.

She loved the second coming and always waited for it. It usually sneaked up on her and was much more powerful than the first. She fell onto her side of the bed.

"Now, you must really be punished," he said.

"No, please … I've been punished enough." She reveled in the warm glow between her legs.

"*I* decide when you've had enough—get on your hands and knees."

She knew what he had in store for her next. Stella couldn't wait for him to shove his cock into her after she had flooded him twice. Norman rammed into her twat, and she screamed from the invasion. He spanked her each time he thrust into her, hitting her butt cheeks until they turned red.

What excited her was the unpredictability of which hole he would choose. One time, he inserted into her ass instead. It was a shocking initiation into anal intercourse, but she let him take her. In a way, she had encouraged it since she let Norman know how much she loved surprises.

"Bad queen," he said as he hit her. "You have disgraced the kingdom. You must realize the consequences."

"Yes," she said, tears streaming down her face from the intensity of his fucking. She reached between her legs and diddled with her pussy as he slammed into her, harder with each stroke.

"Get ready for my golden liquid to fill you up," he said, grunting from the exertion.

"Oh …" She was almost there … almost.

Norman grabbed her ass and plunged into her a final time before he jerked out of control.

"Take that!" he yelled as he blew his wad into her.

"Oh ... oh ...," she cried.

Norman slipped out of her and collapsed on the bed, breathing heavily. "Lick me dry," he said.

Stella was only too happy to oblige. She knelt over him and cupped his balls, lapping up anything that spilled out of his valuable jewels and onto his groin. He sighed and caressed her hair. After several minutes, there was not a trace of semen on his body. Stella lay beside him on the bed.

"My queen, you didn't quite make it, did you?"

"No. I was close, though."

"That's not good enough," he said, sounding almost patriarchal. "Play with yourself, show me what you do when I'm not filling you up."

Norman watched as Stella worked herself up to a third orgasm. She cried out both with ecstasy and exhaustion until she had nothing left to give.

He took her hand and licked the cum off her fingers. "Yes, my queen, I hope you now consider yourself duly punished."

*   *   *   *

Norman Desmond was apparently named after the character Norma Desmond from the movie *Sunset Boulevard*. It was a role made famous by Gloria Swanson—about an aging and narcissistic actress attempting to return to the silver screen after twenty years. Stella supposed the name had a lot to do with Norman going into theater, but in a cruel twist of fate, he discovered he had horrible stage fright. Given that, he went into directing instead.

When she first met him, he was working on a stage play at the Broadhurst in midtown Manhattan. He'd had some success as a director and was well regarded by his peers. A staunch supporter of the Shakespeare Society, he had a lengthy involvement with Shakespeare in the Park and knew many of the Hollywood actors who had performed at the Delacorte Theater in Central Park.

Norman was considered wealthy, the sole beneficiary of a sizeable inheritance from his parents when he was not yet thirty. It allowed him to indulge his creativity in his professional life and his penchant for fun in his personal one. Stella found him attractive. He was forty-nine and had a full head of thick gray hair with a beard to match. He paid meticulous attention to his appearance and dressed his broad six-foot frame in only the best linen suits. With his kind brown eyes and firm lips, Stella thought he could pass for a philosophy professor. In every sense, he was a gentleman, except when it came to sex.

Their first encounter was over lunch at an outdoor coffee shop in Bryant Park. It was a bright day, the air was crisp, and the city was ablaze in red and orange maples. It was early October, and the leaves had just started to fall. Stella wore a sleeveless black dress that showed off her figure, adorned only with a red shawl in case it got cooler later in the day. She recalled that Norman looked pleased with her appearance.

He let her know exactly what he wanted, and he conducted their meeting like an audition for a role. He was a serial monogamist and not interested in multiple partners. He wanted to have fun, but he would not tolerate her having affairs while in a relationship with him. In return, he promised to explore their sexual fantasies, as long as both consented to them. It was something Stella couldn't resist. She didn't see the harm in dating him, and she was certainly not interested in another lengthy commitment.

On their second meeting, Norman invited her to his apartment in the Upper West Side. She had let a few close girlfriends know exactly where she would be in case anything happened to her. She didn't think he was a serial killer, but one could never be too cautious.

Norman had one of those fabulous open-concept condominiums that overlooked Central Park and came with a doorman. Upon first entering, the focal point was a huge espresso-colored three-piece sectional couch in the sunken living room. His place was modern and furnished in contemporary brushed metal and glass. It was decorated with old film posters and black-and-white photographs of New York street scenes. He also collected vintage movie equipment and had cameras scattered around as art pieces. She only later learned that he had state-of-the-art film cameras strategically wired into certain rooms to record sexual activity.

She recalled their first evening together. He had made her a light dinner of salad and angel hair pasta with tomatoes. A meat eater, he had cooked a separate smoked chicken dish for himself. She thought it was considerate of him to prepare something special for her. Afterward, they sat on the couch drinking cappuccinos and talking.

"Stella, I'm a man of unusual tastes. I told you at our first meeting that I'm not prepared to enter into anything short term."

"Yes, I recall your saying that."

"I need a leading lady for at least six months. I think you will find I have a lot to offer."

"Okay, I'm open to that."

"Good, if things work out, we can continue the relationship—if you wish."

"Fine. May I ask what happened to your previous leading lady?"

"Nothing. It just ended. We stopped enjoying one another."

"I see. What would you like me to do?"

"Play along," he said.

"What does that mean?"

"Let's see how well you improvise."

She was confused. Ten years of married life, two years of dating, and now this man was speaking to her in riddles.

"I'll bite," she said. "You start."

Norman got up and did a 360-degree twirl in the middle of his living room before facing her with a totally different expression. He was no longer gentle Norman, and she couldn't figure out if he looked angry or constipated. She almost burst out laughing at how ludicrous he appeared. He, however, was dead serious.

"Queen Stella, will you follow me to my dungeon?" He held his hand out to her.

What did she have to lose? If he was an ax murderer, he certainly didn't have to put on a show for her.

"Yes, my king. I am your willing servant." She was shocked to hear the words come out of her mouth, and she immediately saw that her response delighted him.

They went into what she thought was his bedroom—it wasn't. Instead, it was a room filled with equipment she had only seen in magazines and on the Internet. There were three walls of floor-to-ceiling mirrors. Pushed against the unmirrored wall was a bed, but it was no regular bed. This one had attachments on it made for bondage play. She noticed a bench nearby that looked like something used in a gym for pressing weights. Hanging from the ceiling was a sex swing. There was also an open wooden chest on the floor, containing paddles, floggers, and whips. The room was dim, lit only by a low-watt bulb in a corner lamp.

What the fuck had she gotten herself into? Stella wanted to bolt, but to her astonishment, she felt a warm tingling up her spine at the sight of the room and its contents.

"My queen, this way, if you please."

He guided her to the sawhorse furniture piece she had thought resembled an exercise bench. It had leather-padded cushions with straps and cuffs built into it.

"What is this?" she asked.

"This is a punishing bench," he said. "It's nothing to be afraid of, but you have been a naughty queen, and you need some discipline."

"I …" She was sweating at this point but paralyzed to make a move.

"Take off your clothes, my queen."

He said it so dryly and with such authority that she was hypnotized into obeying. Once she was naked, he was not shy about giving her the once-over. Stella was nervous even though she could tell he liked what he saw.

"Turn around," he said to her in a sharp tone.

Stella did as she was told, but she was anxious. "I—"

"You will enjoy this, I promise you."

He strapped her into the bench. She was kneeling doggie style, her forearms and knees spread apart. Powder-coated steel cuffs locked her wrists and ankles into place. Her midsection was bent over a padded waist bar, provoking her ass to stick up in the air. Once locked in, she was exposed and fully accessible at every entry point. It was the first time Stella had ever felt simultaneously scared and sexually aroused.

"Please don't hurt me, Norman," she said, realizing it was too late at this point to make any demands of him.

"That's *King* Norman." He sounded upset that she had stepped out of character.

"Yes, of course—King Norman, please don't hurt me." Now she was really scared.

Norman was behind her, kneeling between her legs. Though she couldn't see him, she knew his eyes stared straight into her glistening snatch. He inserted a finger into her, and she shrieked—then another, and she let out a lengthy wail. She was vibrating with anticipation.

"I won't be hurting you, my queen, but I am going to punish you until you surrender to me."

"Oh … yes, my king." She was wet as he fondled her, using his thumb to rub her swollen clit.

"How much of my tongue-lashing do you think you can withstand?"

Stella could hardly believe the question, and she did not hesitate to give him an answer. "My king, please lash me until I promise never to disobey you again!"

"And so it is done."

Stella lost count of how many times she came that night. On more than one occasion, she thought she was having an out of body experience. The fear of the unknown had increased her excitement exponentially. She was hooked.

*   *   *   *

Stella loved Norman's insatiable quest for kinkiness. He was a complex man, but he was emotionally available to her whenever she needed him. She enjoyed indulging him, and he generously reciprocated. In many ways, he was the perfect boyfriend. Exploration and sexual gratification were the goals, and they took great pains in testing each other's limits. Both knew how to give and receive pleasure and were not shy in expressing their desires.

She learned early on of his dramatic quirks. He never had sex out of character. His roles were typically those of royalty—a king, a prince, or a lord. He had perfected his Old English accent for these very occasions. During role-playing, it wasn't always easy to decipher where reality ended and fantasy began. He definitely had passive-aggressive tendencies and was able to derive satisfaction as a Dom or a sub.

Despite his eccentricities, he made her happy, and he was exactly what she wanted right now. Stella adored Norman, and she didn't think having a ménage à trois should conflict with that. She required him to be a part of it and decided to bring up the subject again during dinner the next evening. She could usually talk him into anything using the right kind of persuasion.

"We forgot to turn on the movie camera last night," he said to her.

"Oh?"

"Yes, you have to remind me. I must review the footage of us after we've had sex. After all, I'm still perfecting my moves."

"Norman, you were wonderful. I'm not sure you can get any better."

"Oh, of course, I can. After each performance, there must be room for improvement, or else it's not worth doing anymore."

"All right, Norman. If you say so."

She wanted to amuse him, and she needed him in a good mood. "Norman?"

"Yes?"

"You know there's no other man in my life but you, right?"

"Where is this going?" He wasn't easily fooled.

"I just wanted you to know I'd do practically anything for you."

"Really?"

"Yes, I thought this might be the weekend we try something you had mentioned awhile ago."

"Oh? What's that?"

"That little thing involving public mischief?" She raised her eyebrows and threw him a wry look.

"I see, and considering you've been reluctant to pursue that, why now?"

"Oh, I just want to make you happy, that's all."

"Hmm ..." A suspicion of a smile appeared on his face, and he leaned in to kiss her. She tasted the tomato sauce of the lasagna she had prepared.

"Queen Stella?"

"Yes, my king?"

"You're not saying that just because you expect something in return, are you?"

"Well—"

"For example, the threesome again?"

The jig was up. Maybe she wouldn't be able to use her feminine wiles to get her way after all. "Norman, I—"

"That's *King Norman* to you," he said. "And I don't think you've learned your lesson yet."

She knew then that she had him.

*   *   *   *

Norman and Stella sat across from screenwriter Joe Gillis on the couch. It was their second time together, and they had just finished dinner at Norman's condo. A week and a half earlier, they had their first meeting, where Joe was

43

one of four men they interviewed. Norman had agreed to the threesome under one condition—it would happen only once. Stella said she would comply with his wish. He was indulging her fantasy, but he was reluctant. Norman's attitude deflated her enthusiasm somewhat, but not enough to call it off. She didn't know his issues, and he didn't disclose them. Was it because he didn't want to share her? Did he have concerns being with another man? Or was it something else completely? Regardless of what it might be, she let it go, delving instead into finding the right candidate before Norman changed his mind.

Both Stella and Norman liked Joe, but for different reasons. She liked him because he seemed sweet and had a boyish charm. He was also quite handsome, though not in the male model way. He had substance and was not just pretty to look at. Joe was well built, the same height as Norman, and had dark brown hair and eyes to match.

Norman liked that they had similar interests, and he felt an immediate affinity with his name. Joe Gillis was the lead character in *Sunset Boulevard*, played by William Holden. He was a struggling screenwriter who had been ensnared by Norma Desmond to help write the script that would mark her comeback to Hollywood.

It was no coincidence that Joe became a screenwriter. He was a film buff and intimately familiar with the 1950 classic directed by Billy Wilder. He had relocated to New York from Montreal, Canada, only a year earlier. While trying to sell his screenplay, he took acting jobs to pay the rent. Stella could tell he won points with Norman for that, as it showed he had ambition.

Dinner had been casual, and there was a relaxed vibe among them. Of the four men they had met, Stella agreed with Norman that Joe was the most suitable to them. She also knew that Norman understood actors, so she hoped Joe could take direction well. She let Norman lead the conversation tonight as she sat back and listened.

*   *   *   *

"Joe, you're twenty-nine, is that right?" Norman asked.

"Yes, pushing the big three-oh."

"I'm pushing the big five-oh. You're just a kid."

They all had a chuckle.

"Well, Norman, you don't look anywhere near fifty," he said.

Norman accepted the compliment as genuine. "Tell me, what interests you about having a threesome? This is a first for you, right?"

"Yes, that's right."

"Do you consider yourself bisexual?"

"No. I've never pursued an encounter with a man. The thought of it doesn't turn me off, but I love women too much—that's my main interest."

"So a threesome is to get closer to a man?"

"No, not at all, it's to learn how to please a woman better."

"How's that?" Norman was interested now.

"You're obviously an open couple who know what you like. I've had a few girlfriends and been told I'm good in bed, but I want to be certain. I need to learn more about performing from people like you. I'd like to improve as a lover."

Norman saw in Joe a mirror image of himself when he was that age. Even though he was twenty years younger, it sounded like he had similar sexual insecurities.

"Joe, I think that's all very commendable, but my question is—will you be able to please Stella? She's the one we're both here for. This is her fantasy."

"Of course. I understand. And to answer your question—yes, I can please Stella."

"What makes you say that?"

"I'm tuned in to what a woman wants. Like most actors, I listen for cues."

"So you take direction well."

"Yes, I would say so."

"Then you wouldn't mind if I film our scenes to review them later … purely for the purpose of improving technique, of course."

Joe seemed a bit hesitant. "I—"

"Trust me," Norman said. "The film stays within these four walls. You have my word."

"All right, but may I make a request?"

"What's that?"

"I'd like to watch it too."

Norman liked the way Joe's mind worked. It would not have been a deal breaker if he refused to be filmed, but it certainly made it more interesting that he didn't mind being in front of a camera.

Norman grinned. "Yes, that can be arranged."

"All right, then. I have just one last question."

"Sure."

"What's my role?"

*   *   *   *

Stella felt a slight prickling between her legs when Joe said that. She definitely liked how the conversation had progressed. Joe was not aggressive, and he was eager to learn. It was a position Norman was already familiar with—that of director.

Just then, she glanced at Norman, who motioned her to take over.

"Joe, I think I speak for both Norman and myself when I say that we appreciate your honesty, and we want to assure you we are in this for fun. It's a first for us, and it should be an enjoyable experience for everyone, not just me."

"But you're the center of attention."

"Yes, you're right about that." She liked him a lot and was already turned on. "In answer to your question about your role, I'm going to tell you what Norman said to me before we had sex the first time."

"What's that?"

"Play along."

He gave her a puzzled look but didn't ask her to elaborate. As an actor, she figured he should be used to taking cryptic direction. She got off the couch and extended her hand to him. Before he took it, he first turned to Norman, who gave him a nod of approval. Stella liked that Joe was respectful of their relationship.

"Come with me. You have just passed your first test," Stella said. "The king and I would like to see if you're worthy of being promoted within our kingdom."

Joe didn't miss a beat. "Queen Stella, you are my gracious host. I am but a lowly servant to you and the king. I shall do as you request."

As Stella led Joe away, she felt Norman's eyes follow her. Approaching the dungeon, she motioned for Joe to enter first. She turned to see that Norman had not budged from the couch. Before she closed the door, she blew him a kiss, and he winked at her.

*　　　*　　　*　　　*

"Isn't Norman joining us?" Joe asked as they entered the dungeon.

"You mean *King Norman?*"

"Yes, of course. My apologies."

"He'll be here shortly. In the interim, I'll show you some of our toys."

Stella did a walk-through of the equipment in the dungeon, and she could tell from Joe's expression that he had never seen anything like it.

"These are amazing. I—"

"Quiet! He'll hear us."

"What? Who?"

"The king. He doesn't know I'm here with you."

"But we just—" he started, and then realized the game. "I see … Queen Stella, what must we do?"

"If he catches me, I'll certainly be in trouble."

"We don't want that."

"No, we must pretend you have abducted me. I will protect you if he discovers us."

"My queen, if I have abducted you, I would certainly take advantage of you. The king would not believe it otherwise."

She liked his thought process. "You're so right."

"Please get into the swing."

"Do you think that is wise?"

"Yes, the king will surely see you could not have been a willing participant. Let me help you out of your clothes, my queen."

"Yes, we must hurry."

Joe touched her tentatively at first, but he got bolder when she stroked his chest and grabbed his crotch. He was bursting to be released.

He moved to kiss her, and she welcomed him. She kept her hand on his bulge, massaging him, feeling him grow harder. He stuck his tongue in her mouth and darted around her lips as he continued to undress her. He pulled down the zipper on her little black dress and let it fall to the floor. She was left wearing a satin cherry-red open-cup bra and a pair of three-inch red stilettos. Stella was not a big fan of underwear.

He stepped back to look at her. "My queen, you are truly a sight to behold."

Stella was aroused. "Please undress and help me into the swing."

He followed direction very well. When he took off his pants, his penis sprung out and pointed up directly at her. He wasn't as long as Norman, but he was extremely thick. He also had the largest balls she had ever seen. The sight of a new cock made her more wet.

"My queen, please allow me to assist you," he said, strapping her into the swing.

Stella had used the swing many times before, but it was tricky getting into it. Not only did it swing from side to side, but it was also attached by a bungee cord to create a free-floating effect. When she was fully strapped in and suspended, he spun her once and then pushed her into a swinging motion.

"Officer Gillis, I invite you to lick the queen's jewels."

He retrieved a pillow nearby and knelt on the floor, awaiting the swing to come back to him. When it did, he pulled her toward him. "Oh, Queen Stella, you are lovely, simply lovely."

"Enough talking. Suck my hole!"

He did just that. He held her ass and jabbed into her. Stella's weightlessness gave him easy access. He inserted two fingers into her slit, gliding them along her crack as he rubbed her clit with his thumb.

All the while, Stella was swinging from side to side, effortlessly vibrating her plump lips on his face. She locked her legs around him and took full advantage of the spring-like action to force herself upon him.

She was bouncing at a feverish tempo. "Oh, Officer Gillis, please quench your thirst."

He assaulted her with ferocious licks that left her breathless. When she started panting, he spun the swing, fucking her as she twirled on his fingers. When she cried out, he clutched her again and planted himself deep in her cunt, sucking every crevice, moving her up and down on him. He was exceptionally loud as he ate her, and the sounds were almost enough to send her over the edge. Stella felt like she was being devoured.

Joe compressed one of her breasts till she screamed, not from pain, but from the shock it sent directly to pussy. He manhandled the other as well till both her nipples stood at attention. He continued to oscillate his tongue against her.

Stella began to spasm. "Ohhh … I'm coming …"

He stuck a finger in her anus, exerting pressure, and Stella squeezed it with her death grip.

"Oh … my lord!" she cried, as she squirted him with her hot cum. He enclosed his mouth on top of her, slurping up her juices. Stella thrashed about in the swing, reeling from her orgasm. She clamped tightly around Joe's neck as multiple seizures wreaked havoc on her body. He drank her up.

They were both so engrossed in the act that neither of them heard the door open.

*   *   *   *

"What in God's name is going on here!" Norman yelled.

They froze.

Stella was still in the throes of coming and reluctantly pushed herself away from Joe. He got up from his kneeling position and stood facing Norman, his stiff cock in full view. "My king," he said, providing a gentleman's bow in Norman's direction. "Queen Stella and I were—"

"I can see exactly what you and the queen were doing. You need not explain. You will speak only when spoken to."

"Yes, my king," Joe said.

Norman was naked. He was carrying a black flogger with numerous nylon tresses.

"Queen Stella, do you have an explanation for this? What are you doing with my first officer?"

Stella was still basking in her climax and only just beginning to think clearly again. She swayed back and forth in the swing. Seeing Norman standing in front of her with a flogger only made her more excited.

"My king, Officer Gillis abducted me. He forced me—"

"Lies! No one forces you to do anything. My guess is this was your idea."

"I—" She started to protest.

Norman walked over and leered at her hanging in the swing, her face flushed and eyes half-closed. "Look at you!" he said. "You have allowed another man to touch you, haven't you?"

Stella did not answer him.

"Haven't you!" he shouted.

"Yes, I have," she said, barely audible.

"I can see that. You are wet, so wet …"

Stella could see his hunger as he looked at her oozing pussy.

"My king, you are right," she said. "It was not Officer Gillis' fault. Please don't punish him."

"I have no intention of punishing him. I know he was only following orders. If anyone is to be punished, it is you."

"No, I beg of you to spare me."

"Oh, I will spare you, my queen … but you will not soon forget my wrath."

Stella twitched with anticipation.

"Officer Gillis!" Norman turned to Joe.

"Yes, my king," he said.

"Take this."

"Yes, my king." Joe took the flogger and stood beside Stella.

"Whip her!" Norman commanded.

Joe hesitated and looked over to Stella. He tapped her lightly across the chest.

"Harder!" Norman ordered him. "You will obey me, or I will have *you* flogged!"

Joe whipped her again, but with only slightly more force.

Stella could tell he was still tentative, and she wanted to reassure him that it was okay to proceed. "Officer Gillis, please obey the king. I do not wish his rage upon you." She smiled at him with her eyes.

Joe hit her again, and she moaned. Though the tresses left no mark, her breasts were red. He continued to flog her with more confidence across the back, arms, and legs.

"Whip her twat!" Norman yelled.

Joe hit her, and Stella let out an ardent groan. He hit her again, and she jolted up on the swing from the sheer lust of watching these two men fulfill her wildest fantasy. Stella's body sizzled, and every orifice yearned to be filled.

"Enough!" Norman shouted.

Joe stopped flogging her. Her entire groin area was soaked with her fluids. She had practically come again just from the whipping.

Norman walked up to Stella, readjusted the harness and straps, and placed her in a sideways split-leg suspension. He grabbed her top leg and swung it over his shoulder, and in one quick motion, he plummeted into her dripping snatch with his cock. She shrieked from being penetrated so deeply.

He fucked her mercilessly, his balls slapping loudly against her red and scorched pussy. Joe was standing nearby, one hand still holding the flogger, the other, rubbing himself.

Norman eased up on Stella for a moment to address him. "Officer Gillis, you were deceived by the queen as I was. Is that correct?"

"Yes, King Norman, that is correct."

Stella was panting and had been gazing at Joe's perpetual hard-on for a while now. She had no clue what Norman planned next.

"May I suggest you punish the queen for uttering lies?" Norman said.

Stella saw him give Joe a knowing look.

"My king, if you wish, that is what I will do."

"It is."

With that said, Norman resumed fucking her.

Stella was trembling with desire. This was better than she could have ever imagined.

Joe approached her with his boner and held it in front of her face. Stella noticed he kept eye contact with Norman the entire time. There was obviously some kind of unspoken code between them, as she knew they had not discussed anything beforehand.

She grasped Joe with both hands to taste the liquid salt that had seeped from him. She held him firmly, stroking him as he rotated his hips. She tongued his tool from end to end until he was wet and shiny.

Stella licked the underside of his penis at its most sensitive area, where the head meets the shaft. When she felt his fingers in her hair, she immersed herself farther, sucking his velvety balls.

She felt and heard Norman pounding away at her. She glanced to see he had turned into a wild man. She would never have guessed it, but it seemed he got even more turned on when she started giving Joe a blow job.

"Is this what you want, Queen Stella?" Norman said, grunting his words at her. "Two of us—fucking your cunt … and your mouth … at the same time?" He caressed her mound, avoiding her clit but teasing all around it.

Stella nodded toward Norman and batted her lashes. Gripping Joe's cock, she swallowed him only to let go and inhale him again. She picked up the pace as she felt his movements become more volatile.

She was swinging from side to side and bouncing up and down. Zero gravity gave her the freedom to sway in any direction she wanted to derive pleasure from the two men.

"Whip her tits!" Norman commanded Joe.

Joe complied and started whipping Stella across her breasts. She continued sucking him, spiraling her tongue over his rim repeatedly.

When Norman rammed into her, she freed Joe from her gullet. When Norman withdrew, she took Joe deep into her throat. They had a rhythm going, and she heard blood roaring in her ears. She loved how these two men ravaged her, and she knew it would not be much longer before she exploded.

"Queen Stella, no one comes till I say so!" Norman said—the consummate director.

He was fucking her erratically, and she could not recall a time when he felt bigger inside her. Stella was sweating, and her pussy was hotter than molten lava. With her jaw opened wide, her mouth stretched to its fullest, she found it difficult drawing air through her nostrils, yet she couldn't stop. The room was highly charged with the sounds of sex—Stella slurping cock, Norman's testicles slapping up against her ass, and the *thump* of every lash on her body. Her boobs were burning, and her groin muscles were clenching hard and fast.

"Officer Gillis!" Norman called out.

"Yes, my king!"

"We must properly punish the queen."

"Yes, my king!"

Stella found it laughable they had to yell to compensate for their breathlessness. She was on the brink and sensed that both men were there as well.

"I will not tolerate her lies." Norman shouted.

"I understand, my king. What must we do?"

"She deserves a double facial."

"Yes, my king!" Joe nodded.

Norman finally touched her crimson nub, and she lost it. She contracted around him with so much pressure that she was sure he almost shot his semen right then.

The men pulled out of her simultaneously, and she came with a wail that could have woken the dead. She jerked in the swing, her legs flailing about as she spasmed repeatedly.

She cried out with the agony of release, her body a giant ball of electric current. Dizzy from her climax, she closed her eyes for a second. When she opened them again, she found herself staring down the barrels of two loaded cocks.

"Oh …," she gasped, still shuddering from her orgasm. She was barely able to think before she saw them manually stroke themselves one last time and come in unison. The sounds they made were inhuman—two wild animals in heat. Norman squirted before foaming like uncorked champagne, and Joe spurted several long streams and pulsed to a dribble.

Stella instinctively stuck out her tongue to catch the drops that flew in her direction. She reached out to milk their balls to finish them off before taking a dick in each hand. Neither one had any objections to her licking him dry, alternating between the two of them.

*　　*　　*　　*

Stella was having lunch with Jake. She had not seen him in almost a month and wanted to tell him about her threesome.

"No way!" he said when she told him of the wild ride she'd had the night before.

"Yes, it was incredible, Jake. I've never been more aroused in my life."

"You're making me jealous!"

"I don't mean to. You know I can't talk to my girlfriends about this."

"Yeah, the ones who are married, with kids, and don't have sex anymore?"

"I'm not sure about that, but they already think I'm a slut."

"Girl!" Jake said in a high-pitched, affected voice. "Slut is just another word for someone who gets a lot of it, and there's nothing wrong with that—I wish I were a slut!"

Stella looked at Jake with tenderness. He had become a good friend to her after her divorce. He was single and still searching for that special someone, but he had little luck. His appearance had a lot to do with it. Despite his size, though, he was gentle and shy, earning his living as a nurse in a geriatric facility.

"You're the best, Jake."

"I guess there's no chance of turning your threeway into a fourway, is there?"

"Jake …"

"I know. I had to ask."

"No, it's not that. It was just a one-time thing anyway."

"Why's that?"

"It was a condition with Norman before he agreed to be a part of it."

"Is he that insecure?"

"I don't think he is, but maybe he's just a bit intimidated by another man with me."

"Yes, but you're not married to him. You don't have to do everything he says."

"I don't … really. The only thing he wanted was for us to stay monogamous while we're together. Of course, the ménage à trois was different because he was a part of it."

"So why don't you find someone else who wants to swing that way?"

"I don't want anyone else right now. I trust Norman, and we have a lot of fun together. He's the best lover I've ever had."

"Not a stretch from what you've told me about your husband."

"No, really … Norman is fantastic. Sure, my husband was horrible, but I dated many men after him, and those experiences were dismal too."

"I don't see what the big deal is. You're obviously devoted to him."

"You think so?"

"You're kidding me, right?" Jake looked at her with disbelief. "How often do you stay with him at his place?"

"A few days a week."

"You mean from Monday to Friday, home on the weekends to pick up a change of clothes and check the mail, right?"

"Well …" She had to think about it for a moment, but he was right. Stella owned her own house in Brooklyn, but she usually stayed with Norman throughout the week. She rationalized it was more convenient for her to get to her job in the Financial District from where he lived.

"Stella, it's none of my business, but you seem pretty committed to him, so why would he feel insecure about a threesome?"

"It's complex. You've met Norman—he's full of contradictions. I can't figure him out sometimes."

"I think he likes men, and he's afraid to admit it."

"You think he's gay?"

"No, I'm sure he prefers women, but he can get off with a man too. He did with me."

"Right, though he's never said that to me."

"Well, I think he really liked it. I don't remember ever swallowing so much cum."

"Tell me again, exactly, how did it happen?"

"I came by for dinner that night, remember?"

"Yes, I was giving you a half hour to seduce him before I came home."

"There was some chitchat, and Norman brought me into the dungeon soon after I arrived."

"Okay."

"He showed me the equipment, and I was sitting on the bondage bed just checking it out. He stood in front of me and dropped his pants."

"Wait …" Stella never recalled Jake saying that before. "He dropped his pants?"

"Of course he dropped them. How else would I have given him a blow job?"

"No, no, that's not what I meant. I thought you said you helped him off with them."

"What's the difference?"

"Well, I suppose it shows the degree of willingness. I'd assumed he wasn't particularly accommodating."

"Let me just say when he dropped his pants, I knew what he wanted."

"I see, but did you initiate it … or did he?" she asked.

"Well, I thought I did … through you, right?"

"Yes, but … I don't recall saying much to Norman, just that you were my gay male friend who wanted to seduce him, and that he should play along. That's what he always tells me."

"I wouldn't say he played along. It was more like he led the play."

"He just dropped his pants? You didn't have to ask him?"

"I don't know how much clearer I can make it for you, Stella. That's right. He just stood in front of me and dropped them."

"And when you were done?"

"That's when we heard you come in."

"Yes, I remember. I could tell something had happened when you both came out of the dungeon."

"It was an awkward evening, but I chalked it up to Norman getting his first blow job from a man."

"I get that. I just had the impression he was more reluctant about the whole thing."

"Nope, there wasn't much persuasion required on my part."

"Hmm …"

"Does this concern you?"

"I'm not sure."

"You love him, don't you?"

Stella deliberated for a moment. "I do—in an odd way."

* * * *

Stella was having a drink as she waited up for Norman. Her conversation with Jake had started her thinking, and she wanted to get some answers.

Was it possible that Norman had a secret wish to be with a man—and she had inadvertently accommodated him through her fantasy? Was he conflicted because he had enjoyed it?

It was almost midnight when she heard the key in the door.

"Stella, you're still awake?" Norman came in, carrying a satchel and a laptop.

"Yes, how was it?"

Norman had a show scheduled to premiere at the Soho Playhouse Theater in three weeks. He was directing *The Merchant of Venice*. Originally a Shakespeare in the Park production, it was being transferred to Broadway for the fall season. There would be all-day rehearsals three times a week until opening night.

"It went well. We have an excellent cast, and that certainly makes it easier." He glanced at the clock on the wall. "It's late. Don't you have to work tomorrow?"

"Yes, but I don't have to go in early, so I thought we could talk."

"Oh, about what?"

"About yesterday. I'm curious to see how you liked it."

"Yes, we haven't had a chance to talk about that." He walked over to where Stella was sitting on the couch and gave her a warm kiss. "Make me one of those, will you?" he asked, referring to the scotch she was drinking. He dropped his things and flopped on the couch.

"Sure," she said, pouring him a single malt with water, the way he liked it. "You look exhausted."

"I am, especially when I have a vixen like you to keep me on my toes."

"You've taught me everything I know."

"I doubt that," he said.

"Okay, you're right. There's still more to learn." She handed him the drink and sat next to him, her legs curled beneath her.

"Stella ..." He sounded hesitant.

"What is it?"

"You enjoyed yourself with Joe, didn't you?"

"Yes, I did."

"I could see that."

"Norman, it was great. *You* were amazing." She found it difficult to read him. Was he looking for reassurance that he was still her man?

"But Joe was good, wasn't he?"

"Uh ... yes, he was." She didn't want to talk about Joe.

"You liked him, didn't you?"

"Yes, I did, but ..." She paused and then said, "Norman, do you have something you want to tell me?" She was a bit annoyed that he was beating around the bush.

He paused. "I have a small confession to make."

"What is it?"

"I stayed in today after you left."

"Right. You didn't have to go in till later anyway."

"True ..."

"You're making me crazy, Norman. What is it?" She wasn't sure if she was exasperated or anxious, but it was unlike Norman to be this vague.

"After you left this morning, I watched the film of our threesome."

"You did?" She was slightly surprised, but it was hardly anything he needed to confess to her. They usually saw the footage together if they tried something new. Often, their films served as foreplay. "There's nothing wrong with that, so what are you confessing?"

"Stella, at this stage in my life, I thought I had done most of the things I wanted to do sexually. I had always considered myself a one-woman man."

"Yes, I know that."

"The encounter with your friend Jake rattled me."

"How so?"

"It excited me, and I wasn't prepared for that."

"I see. It doesn't imply anything about your sexuality, if that's what you're worried about."

"No, but I did have concerns about being in a ménage à trois, which stemmed partially from that incident."

"Like what?" she asked.

"Like … how would I react with Joe? Would I want him to blow me like your friend had?"

"And?"

"Being part of the threesome reconfirmed that you were the only one who turned me on, not Joe."

"But he didn't turn you off, I hope."

"No, he didn't. I like the guy, but it was more of a friendly feeling toward him—like a comrade or a partner in crime, so to speak."

"Those are interesting analogies," she said. "I thought your reluctance was because you're not keen to introduce a stranger into our games. I know how you don't like getting used to someone new."

"You may be right about that."

"Of course I'm right. It's the same reason you want serial monogamy. Don't get me wrong—that works for me. I don't want a revolving door of relationships either."

"Yes, it takes time to develop chemistry with a person, and I'd have to expose my peculiarities all over again."

"Yes, my king, and you have many of them." She took a sip of her drink.

"Oh …" He reached for one of her breasts.

"Did you like what you saw in our film?" she asked, enjoying the feel of him rubbing her nipple.

"Very much."

"And it turned you on?"

"Like nothing I've ever seen."

"Hmm ..." She noticed the bulge in his crotch.

"Norman, you still haven't confessed anything I don't know."

"I suppose the revelation was how much I liked seeing you with another man."

"Really?" She had already suspected that.

"I also had none of the issues I thought I would have."

"Such as?"

"Jealousy, insecurity, performance anxiety. In the end, I wanted to please you—that's what mattered most. When I saw that he wanted the same thing, I was fine with it."

Stella was wet, and the alcohol had created a sweet haze of heightened arousal. She drank the rest of it and knelt in front of Norman.

"So ... what are you saying, my king?" she asked, unbuckling his belt to tug his pants and underwear down to his ankles.

"I'm open to inviting Joe again ... if you so desire."

"I will do as my king wishes." She couldn't wait to feel him inside her.

"Oh ... my queen."

His cock was throbbing as she held him. She stroked along the shaft and squeezed his balls, seeing him get harder still. He intertwined his fingers in her hair, and she licked around his bulbous ridge.

"My king, should I leave it to you to make the plans?"

"Oh yes ..." Norman's dick was on fire. "Joe will be here Saturday, seven o'clock."

Stella was stunned he had already made the arrangements, but her attention was not diverted for long. She peeked up at Norman who had dropped his head on the back of the couch and closed his eyes. She hesitated just for a moment before sucking him deep down her throat.

*   *   *   *

The workweek dragged on for Stella after she had her talk with Norman.

It was strange how things had unraveled. She had been quite shocked by Norman's change of heart, but she admired his candor and honesty. Unlike her ex-husband, she found him willing to examine himself and talk things over with her. It was what made things work so well between them.

They watched their threesome film together, which led to amazing sex afterward, but there was no more talk about Joe's upcoming visit. There was no point, really. She had adopted Norman's play-along attitude, and it seemed to work fine the first time. Stella was thrilled to have a second ménage à trois with Joe. She liked him, and it was important to her that Norman felt comfortable with him too. She had looked forward to being with the two men all week.

On Saturday, she decided to go back home to take care of a few things before returning to Norman's in the evening. He was making dinner, and Joe was expected to join them. She wanted to feel fresh and relaxed, and she had planned to attend a yoga class, followed by a sauna and Swedish massage.

When Stella arrived at the condo at six thirty, she was puzzled that she couldn't smell the telltale signs of Norman's cooking. He normally prepared exotic meals on the weekends, and she could usually get a whiff of it before even opening the door. She let herself in.

"Norman?"

That was odd. All the blinds were drawn, and it was pitch black in the apartment. She flipped the light switch—nothing.

"Damn," she muttered under her breath. Was it a power failure? If it was, it had to be in his unit only, as she was able to ride the elevator up, and there were lights outside in the hallway.

She made her way into the kitchen to search through a drawer for matches.

"Norman, where are you?"

There was no answer.

She concluded that he probably went out to investigate the power outage. That's all they needed, tonight of all nights.

She found the matches and fumbled her way toward the couch, where she knew there were several pillar candles on the coffee table.

"Don't move."

Stella froze and felt perspiration sweep up her neck.

"What the—?"

"I said don't move—and shut the fuck up." The voice was male, unfamiliar, and right behind her.

"Who are you? Where is—"

She didn't get a chance to finish her sentence. A cloth hood was thrown over her head, and she felt arms on her, grabbing and dragging her. Within seconds, she was lifted off her feet. There were at least two of them.

"Help! Help!" she screamed, struggling with her assailants. The cover muffled her voice, and she panicked. She felt an adrenaline rush, putting her into fight-or-flight mode—her only choice was to fight. She thrashed, kicked, and even tried to bite, but to no avail. They were carrying her somewhere. She heard a door slam and thought she heard voices. She tried to think where she was and felt completely disoriented. She saw a hint of light before she felt herself hurled into the air. She let out a yelp and landed on a bed. She was familiar with the smoothness of the sheets—it was the bed she shared with Norman. When her body hit the mattress, she immediately tried to get up and scramble away, but strong hands held her down, stretching her limbs apart. She heard the click of cuffs around her wrists and felt her ankles being tied with rope. Restrained in a spread-eagle position to the four corners of the bed, Stella tried desperately to shake off the hood.

She heard mumbling. "Who are you? What do you want?" she yelled.

There was no response.

"Are you after money? I can get you money."

No response.

She was terrified. Stella wasn't sure if anyone was still in the room. She heard a door open and close, and then it was quiet. She tried to think, but her mind was too agitated to piece together anything helpful. Where was Norman? She was afraid now something terrible had happened to him. And how about Joe? He should be due any minute …

Stella froze with realization. Joe—she could use him to her advantage.

"Look, please, I have company arriving!" she shouted. "He'll be very worried if I don't let him in."

There was a rustling sound, but she couldn't make it out.

"Hello? Is anyone there?"

She heard nothing.

"I'm telling you the truth. Someone's coming any second. He'll know something is wrong."

Silence.

"Damn it! Is anyone there?"

"Hello, Stella."

Her heart skipped a beat. She was immediately showered in sweat.

"Joe?"

"Cut it off her," he said, his voice devoid of any expression.

"What the fuck?" She screamed like a banshee and twisted frantically in an effort to escape the unknown.

"Stella, be still, goddamn it!"

She heard the sound of scissors—someone was cutting her dress. With her mind racing, she started to feel claustrophobic. What was happening? Where was Norman? What was Joe doing here already?

Stella heard footsteps. They appeared to be leaving the room. She had no clue how many people had been in there. It could have been an army for all she knew.

"Joe, what the hell's going on?"

Silence.

"Joe!" she screeched and sensed a chill over her body. Tied up and fully exposed, she was never more vulnerable in her life. Though confused and distraught with worry, she couldn't help but be aroused. It incensed her to think she could feel turned on at a time like this.

"Joe!" she yelled out again.

She heard movement nearby, and then the head cover was abruptly snatched off her. It took her a few seconds to focus. She was in the bedroom, as she had suspected, bound with cuffs and rope she and Norman occasionally used. Joe stood at the side of the bed. The only light in the room was from several candles on top of the dresser.

"I'm right here, Stella."

"Is this your idea of a sick joke?" she asked.

"It's no joke, Stella. You and Norman invited me here for some fun. I just thought I'd change it up a little."

"What the hell are you talking about? Where is Norman?"

"He's around. The old geezer put up a fight."

Stella felt her nipples stiffen when he said that. "I'll kill you if you hurt him!"

"Is that so?" Joe sat down next to her. "And how do you propose to do that while shackled to the bed … my queen?"

She felt the sting of his words. He was in control now, but of what? She had no clue what his game was.

"What do you want, Joe? Is it money?" She was more angry than scared now.

"You don't give me enough credit, Stella. I want it all. I want Norman's life. He has it pretty good here—this apartment, the dungeon … you." He reached over and touched her—she was wet.

"You animal, take your paws off me!"

"I don't think so, Stella." He inserted a finger inside her. "You like it too much."

She tried to squirm away from him, but he continued to probe her. She closed her eyes, letting out a ragged sigh, trying beyond all hope to hide her excitement as he rubbed her secretions across her pussy.

"Where is Norman? What have you done to him?"

"Don't worry about your precious king. He's … shall we say … tied up at the moment." He inserted another finger inside her.

She compelled herself to stay calm but couldn't deny how he made her feel. Stella wanted to believe Norman was okay. He had to be. This was a bad dream, and she wasn't sure how she ended up here. They had let a psychopath infiltrate their play—a clean-cut Canadian had tricked them with his polite demeanor and artificial eagerness. He wasn't just another actor—he was an exceptional actor.

"What are you going to do?" Stella asked, uncertain she wanted to hear the answer.

"There's so much I want to do to you, I can't even begin to name it all." He extracted his fingers from her, sucked on them, and inhaled her scent. "Stella, you're the sweetest thing I've ever tasted. I'm going to enjoy you tonight—all to myself."

"You bastard."

"Call me what you like, but you'll beg me to fuck you … I promise."

"Look, Joe … or whatever your name is … please let me go. You're right—we invited you here, and no one has to know. Just take whatever you want. I have jewelry, I—"

"Stella, trust me, I *will* take what I want."

He got up to undress. He was in no rush, removing his shirt, his pants, and finally, his boxer briefs. His cock was semi-hard and getting bigger by the second.

Stella was unable to look away from him. Despite the fear for her life, her disdain for Joe, and the unknown whereabouts of Norman—she was dripping.

Joe got on the bed between her legs. "You want me, Stella, don't you?"

"Don't flatter yourself." She was defiant, but she knew her body was betraying her.

"Protest all you want … but I see it," he said, staring at her shiny mound.

"Fuck you."

"You want me, Stella, and you're going to say it." Joe lowered himself in front of her swamp of juices. "Oh, my queen, you are so wet."

"I am *not* your queen." She spat out the words as if they were poison.

"That's fine. You may not be my queen, but you are mine tonight." He spread her wide—diving deep into her slit.

"Get away from me. Get away …" Stella was burning up as she fought to avoid his lips.

Joe fluttered across her clit, sucking her labia and licking her crack from top to bottom.

Stella tried to muffle the sounds coming from her throat, but it was impossible. She turned to liquid as he assaulted her more aggressively. He dove farther into her, and she almost blacked out from the intensity of the sensation. Her moans became louder as she struggled against her restraints, instinctively squeezing Joe each time he plunged into her.

He penetrated her with three fingers and leisurely thumbed her ruby bud. She was clenching him, and her muscles were beginning to contract.

"Tell me you want me, Stella," he said, lingering at the mouth of her swollen pussy.

"Go fuck yourself," she said, determined to maintain an unwavering tone.

"All right." He started to withdraw his hand. "Should I stop?"

"Ohhh …" The room was spinning. She was close … so close … "You're a bastard."

"Do you want me to continue? Yes or no?"

She couldn't think straight. All she knew was she wanted to come, but she refused to plead.

"Yes or no, Stella?"

"Fuck you … fuck you …" Her voice was barely audible. "Fuck … yes."

She heard him take a triumphant breath before he burrowed his face in her cunt again, flicking her hot little nub back and forth. She watched him eat her like a savage. She hated him, yet she wanted him. The conflict was unbearable. She couldn't control herself any longer.

"Oh god …" She whimpered as she writhed against him, desperate for release.

Stella flopped like a rag doll, convulsing while she pulled on the unforgiving cuffs. Just when she thought she had finished coming, she felt another jolt hit her. Joe still had his fingers inside her. She clutched the metal links and held on tight, undulating her body to ride out her climax.

"Stella, you're amazing," he said.

She gasped for air—her mind fighting to formulate an escape plan. How the hell was she going to get out of this? The wheels began to turn as her orgasm subsided.

"Joe …"

"Yes, Stella."

"You win," she said.

"I win? What do I win?"

"I admit I want you."

"Really?"

"Yes, please … I need your dick. I want it so badly." She was talking faster than she could think as her brain tried to assemble some logical thought.

"Is that so?" He did not sound convinced.

"Joe, don't tease me. You know how much I loved it the first time."

"Yes, I do remember that." He moved up and straddled her chest, dangling his cock above her.

She lifted her head to look at him. He was an impressive sight, throbbing and slick, waiting to be satisfied.

He held his penis and swung it over her lips. She curled her tongue around him. He was being cautious with how close he allowed himself to get to her.

"Joe, please … I want you."

He advanced a bit more, extending the length of his shaft across her mouth. She gave him quick darts before licking him with great enthusiasm—loud, wet, and sloppy.

"Oh, Stella, you do that so well."

"Joe, please take off my cuffs so I can hold you. I want to feel you—touch you." She continued to blow him, waiting for him to respond.

"Umm ... I'm not sure that's such a wise idea."

"No, please, I can't suck you properly like this, and I want to so badly."

He had gotten bigger, and she sensed that his oversized balls were aching to explode—she licked them as well.

He got off her, and she could tell he was contemplating his next move. She had to strike while the iron was hot.

"Joe, I'm begging you to release me. I want you. I want you inside me, in my pussy, everywhere."

He reached into the night table and took something out. "You're pretty pissed at me, Stella. How do I know you're not going to bite my dick off?" He dangled the key to her cuffs.

"I want your cock too much to ever do that to you, and you know it." She couldn't believe what she was saying, but she just hoped he did.

"All right, Stella, but your ankle restraints stay on."

It was a victory for her ... and exactly what she wanted to happen. When she had her orgasm, she had tugged hard against her ankle ties. They were made of silk, and she was aware they had some give. Years of yoga had built up both strength and flexibility in her limbs. She knew her right ankle could be freed if she tugged on it just a bit more.

"Please Joe, hurry. I can't wait." Her survival instinct kicked in, and she trembled with anticipation.

He unlocked her left cuff first and then her right. He didn't take his eyes off her for a second. She sat up, rubbing her wrists, and saw him put the metal rings and keys away in the drawer.

Joe got back on the bed, sitting next to her. "Now, Stella, you're going to be good, aren't you?"

"You know how good I am."

He grabbed behind her neck to pull her toward him and planted his lips firmly on hers. His other hand extended to her breasts, compressing her nipples between his fingers. She groaned with the sensation of it, a rush that went directly to her clit. He definitely knew how to push her buttons, but she had to think straight. She leaned closer to him, concentrating on her right ankle, making imperceptible movements to wiggle free.

"Damn it Stella, you make me crazy."

"Oh, Joe ..." She had a tenacious grip on his cock. He kissed her with more force. She responded by lightly biting his lips, buying herself time.

"Stella ..."

"Do you like that, Joe?" she asked, as she masturbated him and felt him grow in her hand.

"Yes ... very much." He kneaded her breasts more aggressively.

"You're so thick, Joe. You're amazing ..."

"Stella, I—"

She jerked her ankle out and kicked him across his left temple—hard. He fell off the bed and lay curled up on the floor. She could tell he was completely taken by surprise.

Stella immediately surged forward to unfasten the rope binding her left ankle. She cursed under her breath, breaking out in a cold sweat as she fumbled with the knot. She glanced at Joe, who was beginning to stir.

"What the ...?" He was dazed.

Her ankle slipped out—free at last. She jumped off the bed, attempted to make a mad dash for the door, and tripped the moment her foot hit the floor. What a bloody awful time to have a leg cramp! She madly scrambled up and hobbled as quickly as she could, regaining some normal feeling to her leg. She grasped the doorknob, turned it, and pulled it open, only to have her body yanked backward. The knob slipped from her hand, and the door flew toward her, slamming against the wall. Instead of running out to freedom, she was being dragged from it.

"No! No!" she screamed, as her body was lifted off the floor and carried back into the room. In a futile attempt to escape, she pummeled and scratched the arms clasping her waist.

Joe threw her on the bed and tackled her. He pinned her petite frame, securing her wrists while her legs thrashed about, trying to push him off her. He wrestled her into submission.

They were both out of breath. Stella had tears running down her cheeks. She continued squirming, but it was impossible to get out from under his weight.

"Stella, Stella, Stella," he said. "I didn't see that coming."

"Get off me and I'll show you again!" she spat.

"You're a ball of fire, so passionate, so ..." He bent down to kiss her.

She recoiled in anger, panting and furious with herself for not moving faster. "Joe, you bastard! Do whatever you want with me. Just answer me one question."

"What's that?"

"Where is Norman? Is he okay?"

She detected something odd in his expression.

"Why don't you ask him yourself?" he said.

*   *   *   *

Norman stood in the doorway. Joe rolled off Stella, and she went running to him.

"Norman!" she cried. She flung her arms around his neck, desperately hugging him. She had never been more relieved to see anyone. "Are you all right? Did he hurt you?"

He didn't say a word. She feared Joe had tied Norman up and beat him, but there was no evidence of that. She stepped back to look at him in the dimness of the room, and he appeared fine. He was naked with an enormous hard-on. She turned and saw that Joe had not budged from the bed. The story wasn't making any sense to her. Her mind was still foggy, but she was beginning to see the light.

Stella seethed as she came to realize this was all an act. She took a step forward and slapped Norman across the face. The sound reverberated across the room.

"How could you? I was afraid something terrible had happened to you!" She heard Joe stir behind her but guessed he thought better than to come to Norman's defense.

Norman looked at her with lustful eyes, rubbing the sting off his cheek. "I deserve that, Stella ... I really do, but you forgot one thing."

"What the hell are you talking about?" She could not remember ever being more infuriated.

He stared her straight in the eyes. "My queen, you forgot to play along."

He grabbed her around the waist, savagely compressing her lips with his.

Gasping from the brutality of his kiss, Stella struggled to push him off her. Norman bent her backward and bit behind her ears down her neck, all the while crushing her boobs. She wanted to stay angry and hate him for what he did, but she couldn't. His cock nudged against her stomach, and she felt weak. Her emotions had swung from fear to anger to arousal in a matter of minutes.

He swept Stella up and carried her to the bed. Norman lay next to her, and Joe snuggled up on the opposite side. It was as if she had just experienced the worst lover's quarrel in history, and it was now time to make up.

"Both of you are bastards, you know that?" She quivered as she felt herself sandwiched between the two men. Joe was teasing her nipples, sucking on them until they stood up dark and pointy. Norman was kissing her navel and sliding lower.

"We are bastards, no doubt," Norman said. "But we promise to make it up to you … if it takes all night."

Stella was still lightheaded as Norman spread her open and licked her gently, as if to appease her.

"Please forgive me, Stella," he said. "I'm so sorry." He tongued her deeper.

"Oh, I don't know …" Her body had been one tense muscle for the last hour, and she needed desperately to unwind.

Norman threw her legs over his shoulders and ate her more aggressively, repeatedly poking her with his hard tip. She was almost there when he got up and repositioned himself. He turned her onto her side and lay behind her, pushing his cock into her warm hole. Stella started to purr, and he growled in her ear. He reached around and grabbed her tits. His other hand went between her legs, diddling her clit.

Joe had stepped off the bed, waving his boner in front of her. She invited him to come closer and caressed him.

As Norman fucked her from behind, she took Joe's dick in her throat, giving him the blow job she knew he had been waiting for. He moved his hips in harmony with her. Stella felt tiny ripples coming from his balls when she touched them.

"No, Stella …" Joe said. He extracted his prick with painstaking reluctance and stepped back, gripping it firmly near her face. He obviously wasn't ready to finish yet, and she sensed how much he yearned for her.

"Oh …" She was on the edge, but she too wanted to wait.

"Stella," Norman said. "Are you all right?"

"Never better." She was on the verge of a spasm and seized the opportunity to direct the next scene. "Norman, I want to sit on you," she said.

"Whatever you say, my love." He pulled out and rolled over. She couldn't resist his thick rod and gave him a few licks. As she knelt over him, Joe took advantage of her ass sticking up in the air. He separated her butt cheeks and inserted two fingers into where Norman's cock had just been—fucking her, spanking her buttocks at the same time.

Stella was going crazy, but she managed to move away from Joe's stinging slaps to face Norman and straddle him. She sat down, and he totally filled her up. She gyrated her hips, and felt his smooth, hard glide before she gazed at Joe.

"Let me taste you just a little bit more," she said.

She took Joe in her mouth and let him control how much he wanted to give her, continuing to swivel her hips on top of Norman. After several agonizing minutes, during which time Stella thought the men were dangerously close to coming, she let go of Joe.

"I want you both inside me," she said. She looked to Norman, and he didn't object. Stella bent forward and leaned in to nibble Norman's earlobes, her breasts almost resting on his chest—her bottom inviting Joe to take her.

"You heard the lady, Joe. Condoms and lubricant in the second drawer," Norman said.

Stella guessed from Joe's hesitation that it was something he had never done before. She realized he needed a bit of prompting and encouragement to proceed. "It's okay, Joe. It's going to be good for both of us, I promise."

When he came up behind her, he tentatively put his hands on her butt cheeks. She felt him carefully drill into her, grunting when he had the full length of his cock up her tight, puckered hole.

Stella had experienced double penetration with Norman and a dildo, but the feeling of two penises in her was like nothing she had ever felt before. She was beside herself as Norman fucked her from below, and Joe rammed her from behind.

Norman was sweating from exertion, but he was insatiable. He caught one of Stella's dangling nipples and sucked it between his lips. She shoved her boobs into his face to give him more.

Joe had found his rhythm. He was gliding his tool in and out of her like a piston. He began to spank her again, and it made her buck harder against him. She cried out with every smack. The heat Joe created on her buttocks radiated to her pussy, which only made Norman feel hotter inside her. She sensed Joe being squeezed to his limit and guessed he wouldn't be able to last much longer.

Stella fell into a trance of their bodily pulsations and beastly sounds. She loved having both men simultaneously in her. The combination of their thrusting motions brought her closer and closer to the edge until it was impossible for her to hold back. Starting at her toes, she felt a tiny spark grow into a wildfire, burning her up at lightning speed.

"Fuck me!" she screamed, experiencing the most euphoric explosion of her life.

Almost immediately after that, Norman, who had been pumping her steadily, shot his entire load into her. His ass practically sprung off the bed as his thunderous orgasm overtook him. She knew Norman's jerky climax would push Joe to the limit—it did. Seconds later, Joe blew his wad.

*　　　*　　　*　　　*

"To us," Norman toasted, raising a glass of mimosa.

"To us," Stella echoed. "Was it really necessary to ruin one of my favorite dresses?"

"That was Joe's idea. It was touchy for me, but in the end, I think it achieved the effect we wanted."

"It sure did," Joe said as he came to the table.

"You're buying me a new dress," she said.

Joe grinned at her. "It would be my pleasure."

It was Sunday morning, and Joe had volunteered to make breakfast. He was the first to get up after their all-night debauchery, as Norman had referred to it.

"Exactly what *was* the effect you were going for by destroying my dress?" Stella asked.

"Fear," Joe responded. He set down plates of eggs, bacon, and toast in front of them and returned to the kitchen.

"Smells great, Joe." Norman chimed in. "I'm starving."

Stella discovered that the two men had collaborated on the events of last night. Joe had written the script with input from Norman who was aware of Stella's fondness for surprises. Their purpose was for her to have fun, but to also give their play an edgier feel. The scenario was certain to inflame Stella's emotions, and they felt it would ensure she stayed engaged and turned on. What they didn't anticipate was for her to deviate from the script.

Joe came to the table with Stella's oatmeal and commented on that very thing. "Stella, you pack a mean wallop with that leg of yours."

"You're lucky I couldn't swing with full force, or you would have been comatose," she said.

"I don't doubt it." Joe rubbed the side of his head, where she saw a shadow of a bruise forming.

"How many of you were in the apartment when I arrived?" she asked.

"Just us and my friend Bruce," Norman responded. It was his voice you heard in the dark when you first came in. It was Joe and I who carried you into the room. Bruce left after we had you tied down."

"Somehow it seemed like there were ten men with all the footsteps I heard."

"That was the reason for keeping you in the dark. It created that extra element of fear of the unknown," Joe said. "I figured that would heighten the excitement for you."

It certainly had. She had drifted in and out of consciousness throughout their evening after being fucked and sucked in more ways than she ever thought possible. Norman had gotten another erection. She couldn't even remember how many times Joe got it up. There was no limit to what they wouldn't do to please her. As Norman had promised, it took them all night.

At breakfast, they talked openly about their play. It made for a stimulating conversation. After Joe left, Stella lay on the couch with her head in Norman's lap.

"I noticed something different about you yesterday," she said, looking up at him.

"What was that?"

"You were not in character."

"I wasn't?"

"No, you were actually yourself during sex."

"Hmm …" Norman stroked her hair. "That may be a first. I don't think I've *ever* been myself during sex."

"You seemed fine with it though."

"It really didn't cross my mind. I was just concentrating on pleasing you."

"I know. I felt it."

"I guess I've grown quite fond of you, Stella." He bent to kiss her.

"Well, I was hysterical when I thought something had happened to you."

"Yes, I was watching you while the scene was being filmed."

She sat up and glared at him. "Don't scare me like that ever again. It wasn't funny." Her voice threatened, but her eyes were glassy.

"I promise," he said, giving her a peck on the forehead.

Stella felt real affection from him. "So where do we go from here, Norman?"

"Wherever you wish, Stella."

"And Joe?"

"He's always welcome, provided we're all able to play along."

winter

the norwegian

Leah arrived at Cedar Valley the week of Christmas. The resort was located three hours north of Toronto, just a short drive from Algonquin Park. It was comprised of ten log cabins of varying sizes—all with wood-burning stone fireplaces. Hers was considered a luxury cottage, equipped with an indoor sauna and a hot tub on the back deck. Normally reserved for six people, the owners had offered her a deal, as winter was low season, and she had booked it for a full two months.

It was her second night there, and she had just finished dinner when she heard footsteps coming up her walkway. Since there were no phones in any of the cabins, she assumed it was the woman from the front desk. She went to answer the door, and her heart skipped a beat. She'd come face-to-face with a ghost.

At the entrance was a man who stood about six feet two. He had chiseled features and dark, messy hair with just a trace of gray, which he wore short on the sides and longer on top. His ski jacket was lightly covered in snow.

"Hi, I'm Henrik Kristiansen. I'm staying at the Night Lark," he said.

"Henrik …" The color drained from her cheeks.

"Are you all right?" he asked.

"I … Yes, you just caught me off guard."

He stood outside her cabin named Raven. That was the funny thing about Cedar Valley—all the cabins were named after birds. She was staring again.

"I'm so sorry. I'm Leah—Leah Jones." She shook his hand.

"Nice to meet you, Leah."

"I'm being rude. Would you like to come in?"

"Only if I'm not disturbing you."

"No, not at all." She quickly composed herself.

"Sandra at the front desk said we're the only two guests here." He brushed the snow from his jacket, hung it up as he walked in, and stepped out of his boots. "I thought I'd come over and introduce myself."

"Of course, I was just about to have some wine. Would you care to join me?"

"Yes, that would be nice."

She went to the kitchen to get a bottle and a couple of glasses, still tingling from his touch.

"I didn't expect to see anyone else here," he said as he sat down on an oversized chair.

"I was thinking the same thing, especially with Christmas just around the corner."

Leah gave him the drink and sat across from him on the loveseat. She couldn't get over the resemblance—his voice, the way he pronounced her name as *Lay-ah* instead of *Lee-ah*, and then there were those lips. She took a sip of wine to calm down, feeling the effects of its heat immediately. She hoped he didn't notice her blushing.

"How long are you here for, Leah?"

"Till the end of February."

"An extended holiday?"

"Actually, no. I'm here to work."

"Oh? What do you do, if you don't mind my asking?"

"I'm a writer, though lately I haven't been able to write much. I'm hoping to find some inspiration here." She took a bigger sip this time.

"Would I know any of your books?"

"I'm not sure." Leah would have to reveal her pen name—that was unavoidable. "I write as H. J. Carlsen."

"So, *you're* H. J. Carlsen!"

"That's me."

"A good friend of mine is a big fan of spy fiction and has read all your books."

"Yes, I have a spy series, but most of the time, I write adventure thrillers."

He furrowed his brow. "For some reason, I always thought the author was a man, a Norwegian for that matter."

"Yes, but only someone like you would know that."

"What do you mean?"

She hesitated. "You're Norwegian, aren't you?"

"What gave it away? My accent?" His dark eyes twinkled.

"Yes, and I'm aware that *Henrik* is a common Norwegian name." She didn't care to elaborate, opting instead to change the subject. "And you, how long are you here for?"

"Just till after Christmas, I'm working on some training nearby."

"Training?"

"Yes, biathlon. I'm developing a program for Canada's top biathletes. Hopefully, they'll be able to improve their standing at the next World Cup."

"I see. They do have excellent ski trails in this area."

"Yes, they do."

"Do you compete as well?"

"I'm retired now. My last race was eight years ago in Salt Lake City."

Leah remembered that well. "You were in the Olympics? Wow! How did you do?"

"Second in the individual event," he said casually.

"Now I'm *really* impressed."

Leah recalled being glued to the television during those two weeks in February 2002. The biathlon races especially inspired her. She marveled at the endurance and concentration it took to combine cross-country skiing with the ability to shoot targets accurately over a twelve-mile course.

"Did you make all your targets?"

"Yes, I'm an expert marksman. My skiing was where I could have been a fraction of a second faster. A countryman and friend won the gold, so it was a great victory."

"Yes, now I remember you—gold and silver. It put Norway on the map."

"It was sweet."

So was he. A day's growth of stubble could not hide the same striking features she remembered from so long ago—the straight nose, strong jawline, and that mouth. She shivered as she recalled how those full lips felt on her body. Henrik's presence in the room turned her on, even though she tried desperately to push those thoughts aside. When he smiled at her, she dissolved deeper into the couch. She knew he was not the same man—he was older—but the likeness was uncanny.

"You're planning to spend the holidays here by yourself?" Henrik asked.

"Yes, I've had this dry spell for the last six months. I needed to leave Toronto."

"I see, but what about family and friends?"

"What about them?" she said tersely.

"It's Christmas. You shouldn't be alone."

Leah hoped she didn't sound too defensive. She didn't tell Henrik she was not a fan of the holiday anyway—not anymore. She had stopped celebrating it four years ago. Her friends understood and had given up trying to change her mind about it. Her mom, however, was not too happy. Leah was an only child, and Christmas was a huge deal when she was growing up. The family tradition included turkey dinner with chestnut stuffing, cranberry sauce, and rum cake for dessert. It was one of the few times each year that her family got together. Since Leah no longer stayed in the city for Christmas, her mother celebrated with her stepfather's family instead.

For past Christmases, she had gone to a meditation retreat and had no contact with the outside world for two weeks. By the time she returned home, the holiday festivities had wound down, and she was able to focus on writing again. This time, having missed the deadline for her latest thriller, she chose to book the trip to Cedar Valley. It helped her escape two things—the city in holiday chaos and the wrath of her publisher. She had not expected company here … and certainly not someone like Henrik.

Her hope was to seclude herself at the pristine location and get her creative juices flowing again. At that moment, though, the only juices flowing were from her pussy as she shifted in her seat to allay her arousal.

Henrik looked at her with an inquisitive expression. As irrational as it seemed, she almost feared he could read her mind. There was a pause in the conversation, and Leah found herself blushing again, something she did when she was nervous. She was unable to finish her wine.

"Are you all right?" he asked, helping her steady the glass as she put it down on the table. His fingers brushed against hers and sent a pleasurable tremor up her arm.

"I'm fine, really—just a little tired."

"I'm sorry to have dropped by uninvited. I would have called, but they don't have phones here."

Leah immediately felt bad. She was not trying to get rid of him. "I kind of like that there are no phones—it forced you to come and meet me."

"Good point," he said, grinning to show a perfect row of teeth. "I should get back anyway. I have an early morning."

"Training?"

"Yes, six o'clock sharp at the firing range."

Leah walked him to the door. It took all her strength not to reach out and touch him. Though she knew Henrik was flesh and blood, there was still a part of her in denial.

He got dressed, pausing before turning to her. "Leah?"

"Yes?"

"Would you like to have dinner with me tomorrow evening?"

"Dinner? I—"

"That is, unless you have other plans."

"No ..." She took a deep breath.

"I'm sorry," he said. "I'm being too forward."

"No ... I mean, no, I don't have any other plans."

He stepped closer to her. "Is that a yes, then—for dinner?"

His proximity unnerved her, and she couldn't believe how awkward she sounded. "Yes ... okay."

"How's seven o'clock at my place?"

"That's fine. Can I bring anything?"

"Just yourself."

Henrik stepped outside, and giant snowflakes landed on his hair, glistening in the moonlight before disappearing. It was snowing more heavily now. A strong wind hit her, but Leah didn't feel it. She was still burning up.

"Good night, Leah. Hope your writing goes well tomorrow."

"Thank you," she said, shutting the door behind him.

She had not felt desire in a long time, and she found it difficult to watch him leave. It was eerie to know that Henrik made her feel the way she did more than a decade ago—on the day she met the only man she ever loved.

*   *   *   *

Leah had always wanted to travel, but she didn't set foot on European soil till she was almost twenty-six—a gift to herself for finishing her studies a year early. She had completed a combination PhD program in English literature with a master's in creative writing. Her goal was to pursue a tenure-track teaching post at a North American university.

Attracting men was never a problem for Leah. Her curly shoulder-length auburn hair and large green eyes usually caught their attention. Standing five feet six with a curvaceous figure, she stayed fit by doing aerobics, Wii Sports, and eating healthy. Even in the winter, she tried to get outside for some outdoor activity, although she was not a fan of the cold.

While completing her studies, Leah deliberately chose not to make time for men. She liked them enough but didn't find much enjoyment in going out with them. At one point, she went as far as seeing a doctor about her lack of interest, thinking she had a problem with low sex drive. Her doctor found nothing wrong with her and suggested she take an iron supplement.

Leah eventually self-diagnosed the problem as being more psychological than physical. The men she met were just not as exciting as the ones she read about. She could pick up any book by Jules Verne or Alexandre Dumas and experience greater sensual pleasure than going out on a date. For her, even curling up with stories from contemporary writers like Robert Ludlum and Clive Cussler were preferable to boring male contact. Given that, she concentrated on getting her degrees and chose to live vicariously through her books.

Leah met Johan on her last day in Innsbruck—the final city she was visiting in Austria as part of her trip across Europe.

It was January, perfect weather for skiing, and she had spent the day on the cross-country trails. Later, at the après-ski, she was in a restaurant struggling with her high school German to ask the waitress about the menu. Johan walked in and sat at the table next to her. There was instant chemistry when they saw each other. She recalled how he introduced himself.

"Please call me *Yo-hawn*. May I be of assistance to you?"

She had been trying to find out if there was hot apple cider on the menu. He immediately translated for her. Well over six feet tall, he nonchalantly brushed back his matted blond hair and joined her. He hadn't asked permission to sit at her table, but she didn't care. She was lost in his chocolate-brown eyes and couldn't stop staring at him. When he licked his lips, she wondered what it would be like to kiss them.

Johan was twenty-four, an engineer, and spoke fluent German. He was also familiar with several other languages, and his English was excellent. A thrill seeker from Bergen, Norway, he made her feel alive. She wasn't sure if it was the crisp Austrian air that day, or the aroma of the cider he ordered for her, but Johan aroused her as no man ever had.

He possessed the qualities she loved in the men from her favorite books: he was passionate, full of adventure, and above all—fearless.

After she met Johan, Leah changed her itinerary. She had planned to fly to Spain to end her vacation in a warm country. Instead, she spent it in Switzerland, where Johan had booked a heli-skiing trip. He was an expert downhill racer and snowboarder but always on the lookout for the next big thrill in his sport. Though Leah did not ski with him, she went along for a helicopter ride and remembered how her jaw dropped upon seeing a view of the iconic 13,000-foot Eiger North Face. She knew it was not something many people got to experience.

Most of their days were spent apart. Johan was either heli-skiing or heli-boarding while Leah went cross-country, toured the nearby town of Grindelwald, and tried out different spa treatments. During the evenings, however, they were inseparable. He was as fierce in bed as he was on the slopes. After an exhausting day of skiing, Leah was amazed he had the stamina to make love to her.

She recalled one of their last nights together on that trip. Johan had fallen on one of his runs and injured his back. He was in agonizing pain and even walked with a slight limp, yet he refused to seek medical attention. She had planned a horse carriage ride through their small Swiss village, but she had to cancel it. Instead, Leah decided to give him a massage with one of the essential oils she had purchased at the spa.

That was the first time she noticed the scar—a five-inch line running across his right shoulder blade. He told her it was his lucky scar, sustained from a cross-country skiing accident when he was a teenager. It was what made him decide to switch to alpine skiing—a sport he much preferred.

By candlelight, she spent half an hour trying to knead the knots out of his back. She used an oil infused with healing peppermint, which she learned was helpful for sore muscles. Straddling him just below his bum, she moved her hands from his buttocks upward, applying pressure with her thumbs along each side of the spine toward his neck.

When she felt he had loosened up a bit, she asked him to turn over and was stunned to see an erection. It was obvious he was no longer interested in continuing the massage. She saw how he lusted for her, but she was afraid to hurt him.

"Leah, I have a slight pain in my back, but I have no problem with my tongue, and there is certainly nothing wrong with him." He nodded in the direction between his legs. "Take off your clothes and come here."

He had a way with words that turned her on to no end. It was a mixture of his Norwegian-English and his self-assuredness.

"Kneel on top of me, my lovely Leah."

That was his name for her—*Lovely Leah*. She remembered spreading her legs astride his face and lowering her sex over his mouth. She held on to the headboard and swiveled her hips above him, allowing herself to be fully explored.

He caressed her pussy slowly, fondling her slit from front to back. He alternated between his fingers and his tongue inside her slippery hole, working her into a frenzy until she wasn't able to take it anymore. Then he withheld his touch, teasing her, barely breathing on her, until she squirmed in agony and begged him to lick her again.

She couldn't get enough of him this position. It enabled him to flutter his lips against her exposed clit in a way that drove her crazy.

After Johan repeatedly jabbed her with his hard tip, she came wildly, dizzy from her frantic movements. He continued sucking her as she cried aloud, her body writhing as wave after wave hit her. Leah's vocal orgasm always incited Johan. He flipped her on her back as she was still coming and impaled her with one mighty thrust. There was certainly no sign of any sore muscles when he fucked her. That night, he made love to her for hours. Even Johan was shocked at how she had "cured" him. The next day, he was back up on the slopes without any trace of an injury.

Johan was like that. He was not one for half measures in anything he did. He lived for pleasure and excitement. Those qualities made Leah fall in love with him, but they also made her cautious. She was content to have an extended long-distance relationship to make certain they had more than just a fleeting romance. After several years together, and numerous visits to one another's hometowns, they decided they were ready to get married.

Leah was teaching at the time in Toronto but writing as well, completing two full-length novels. She submitted them to a friend and editor, who encouraged her to get an agent. Within six months, Leah received her first publishing deal and an advance for two additional books. Her stories were fiction, and Johan was her muse. She wrote about a man who sought adventure, interweaving her plots with intrigue and sex. She crafted the story lines to parallel the life she dreamt of with Johan. Following the success of her first four books, she gave up teaching altogether. Given that her career was more flexible, she began planning the process to relocate to Norway. She had already enrolled in a language course and was checking into emigration requirements.

Leah arranged for Johan to come to Toronto for a prewedding celebration before Christmas, prior to getting married in Norway. They had planned the wedding for the second week in January, in the year she was to turn thirty-two. For their honeymoon, they wanted to go back to Innsbruck, where they'd first met.

*   *   *   *

Leah had never heard of ski-BASE jumping until after a trip Johan took to the Dolomites in Italy. It was an extreme sport that combined skiing and BASE jumping—an activity that used a parachute to jump from fixed objects. She remembered listening to Johan after he made his very first jump. He told her how he skied off the cliff, popped a parachute strapped to his back, and glided to the ground. He said it was like flying, and he had never felt such a rush in his entire life. It immediately became his new favorite sport, and he tried to do as many jumps as he could.

While they were making their wedding arrangements, Johan had already booked a trip to Switzerland to ski-BASE jump off the Eiger. He planned to fly to Toronto immediately after his trip for the celebration. Leah talked to him the morning before he was scheduled to jump. She heard in his voice how psyched he was. The Eiger would be the highest structure he had ever jumped off. She felt both thrilled and terrified for him.

*   *   *   *

Leah arrived in Bergen with her mother. Johan's brother, Karl, was there to meet them at the airport. He had been there for Johan's last jump. The death was ruled accidental—a parachute malfunction. It was just weeks before Johan's thirtieth birthday.

Leah didn't need an explanation, but Karl insisted on giving her the details, so she let him. She also didn't want to see Johan's body before he was laid to rest. She required none of that for closure. She had come to Bergen out of respect for his family and friends … and to say good-bye.

In her final conversation with Johan, he had told her how much he loved her and how he couldn't wait to spend the rest of his life with her. With those words, she knew he had never been happier when he made his jump. In the end, he did what he loved to do.

When she returned to Toronto on Christmas Day, she sent an e-mail to her editor requesting all her books now be written under the pen name of H. J. Carlsen—Henrik Johan Carlsen. It was a dedication to the man she loved … and her way of keeping his adventurous spirit alive.

For the next three days, she couldn't stop crying.

*   *   *   *

Following Johan's death, Leah immersed herself in her writing. Ideas came at her from every direction, and words spilled out faster than she could type them. Stories seemed to formulate themselves onto pages with little effort from her. Working at a manic pace for six months without taking a break, she completed two books. Her publisher was amazed by her productivity but insisted she take a break before she burnt out.

Over the next several years, Leah wrote incessantly. She usually had multiple ideas on the go, and at one point, had two bestsellers out simultaneously.

The pressure to keep writing meant Leah had no social life—which was fine with her. On occasion, she went out with girlfriends, but many of them were now married with children, and they had their own lives to keep them busy. Dating infrequently, she compared every man to Johan. No one ever measured up. She became somewhat of a recluse again, living through her books, creating stories around what could have been her life with Johan.

Henrik's innocent visit had wreaked havoc with her peace of mind. She had not heard that name in so long, and Johan had rarely referred to himself by his first name. Leah was not one to believe in parallel lives, nor in coincidences, but she couldn't fathom why this man would show up on her doorstep, today of all days—exactly four years after Johan died.

After Henrik left, she had taken a cold shower but was still on fire. She turned out the lights and double-checked the locks.

Leah was unable to fall asleep. She lay in bed physically tired, but her mind was fully alert. With thoughts of Johan, Henrik, and ghosts, the quiet retreat of Cedar Valley no longer felt peaceful—it felt haunted.

She heard the sound first. She guessed it was the blustery wind against the trees, but then she saw someone or something moving in the room. She was paralyzed with fear. It was a faceless apparition. When she opened her mouth to scream, her voice stuck in her throat.

Shadows danced on the walls as the figure slowly approached her, avoiding the beam of moonlight streaming into her room. She had been feverish when she came to bed, lying naked without a blanket. Now she wanted to hide her body, but she had no strength even to reach for the bedsheet. She was fully exposed.

Terrified but also tempted by this phantom presence that was now between her legs, Leah felt her buttocks elevated off the bed. She was immediately overwhelmed by ravenous licks. She let out a groan as the intensity of the assault increased. Leah welcomed it—she desperately wanted it. She spread her legs farther apart and imagined some primitive beast devouring her. Her breathing became shallow as the invasion of her snatch continued. She felt like she was being eaten alive.

Off in the distance, she heard an unfamiliar popping sound. A few seconds later, she heard it again, only this time it was louder and closer. For some unknown reason, she concluded that it was gunfire. She couldn't focus on it, though, as each shot was punctuated by several jabs to her clit from a skillful tongue. She undulated with passion. One last nudge and her body convulsed off the bed as if it were being electrocuted. She heard a roar in her ears and realized it was her own voice, a wild thing, whimpering and mindless. There was another blast. It echoed from just outside her bedroom window.

Leah woke up shaken and slick with sweat. She frantically surveyed the room but saw nothing out of the ordinary. The only sounds were her own halted gasps and the cracking of tree limbs. Covering herself with the blanket, she tried to recollect what had happened, but her memory was fading fast. She curled into a fetal position and touched her pubic area—she was oozing.

Leah suddenly felt vulnerable staying in a remote area without even a cell phone. She kept listening for any unusual sounds outside her cabin, but she heard nothing. Feeling ill at ease and physically spent, Leah fell into a restless sleep.

*   *   *   *

It was still snowing heavily the next morning when Leah got up. The forecast called for a blizzard and eight more inches by the end of the day. As she stepped out to get some extra logs for the fireplace, gale force winds almost blew her off her feet. White powder whirled around her, causing poor visibility. She found the firewood piled high against the side of her cabin, sheltered from the snow by an awning. Leah was outside for less than ten minutes, but her face stung from the intensity of the cold.

After building a fire and having a quick breakfast, she sat down to work, but found it difficult to concentrate—her mind was preoccupied with thoughts of Henrik. Leah knew it was impossible to write when she felt so agitated, so she began by rereading and editing the few chapters she had written so far. Once she was finished with that, she struggled with formulating ideas for new material and ended up deleting half of what she'd already written. Not only was the book not progressing—it was regressing.

Leah was terrified by her writer's block. It was a horrible feeling to stare at a screen after working for hours and not read a single paragraph she was pleased with. The more she persisted, the less she was able to come up with the right words. Leah closed her laptop in frustration—it was another unproductive day.

Due to bad weather, she decided not to go for a walk, something she had intended to do daily at the resort. Growing up in Canada, Leah knew she had to either embrace winter or be destined to live as a hermit until spring. She enjoyed cross-country skiing, but it wasn't convenient to get to some of the better trails. Those were located at least an hour's drive outside the city. She had to make a real effort to get out in the cold for exercise. Working six days a week, that wasn't always feasible.

About two years ago, a friend introduced her to Wii Sports, a video game. It used a motion sensor remote to control the actions of an on-screen character called an avatar. Initially, she thought it ludicrous playing a video game at her age—and equally absurd to use it as a replacement for real exercise. Soon, however, she was hooked, especially during winter, when she craved a workout and wasn't able to get outside.

Leah's favorite was the boxing game because it gave her an excellent cardiovascular session. She boxed holding a Nunchuk, an attachment that allowed her to control her avatar, moving it in a similar manner to how she would punch someone in real life. She fought against the computer-generated opponent in a boxing ring, surrounded by a cheering audience.

Changing into a sports bra, yoga shorts, and a pair of sneakers, she turned on the TV and video game. She muted the television volume and put on music instead. Leah loved exercising with loud music, and she had brought her iPod, preprogrammed with a few thousand songs. She chose a specific set list she'd made called "Boxing to the Eighties." It contained only upbeat dance music guaranteed to get her jumping. She aimed to exercise for at least an hour before dinner at Henrik's.

After her workout and shower, Leah fussed over what to wear. She had not expected to go anywhere fancy while staying at the resort and had only packed casual clothes. In the end, she chose the one top that could pass as semi-dressy—a burgundy silk blouse—wearing it with a pair of black dress pants. She threw on her full-length goose down coat, gloves, and boots and set off to Henrik's cabin.

It was a marvelous night. The air smelled fresh and clean, and a sea of shimmering white surrounded her. It was still snowing, but fortunately for her, the wind was at her back now. She saw her breath as she trudged the winding ten-minute trail to the Night Lark, located across a hill and past several smaller cabins. She saw a cottage named Snowgoose and a tiny one called Hummingbird not far behind it. The pathway was dimly lit until she reached an open area where the main lodge was located. She decided to go in and inquire about the gunshots she had heard.

Leah didn't glean any helpful information from the clerk at the desk. He had only arrived that morning, and the owners were not due back until the day after Christmas. He promised he would bring it up with them when they called later to check in.

She arrived at Henrik's a little before seven. Not wanting to appear too eager, she decided to walk a bit more to see the rest of the area. His cabin was located about one hundred feet from the frozen shoreline of Peninsula Lake, sheltered by numerous conifers. The wind had started to pick up again, and she felt the biting cold of the night air. She stood still, gazing at the stars, and saw a nearly full moon. Inhaling the cold into her lungs, she shuddered, and her mind wandered to a previous winter—a special day she had spent with Johan.

It was during one of his trips to Canada that they decided to go tobogganing at a conservation area an hour outside of the city. It was a bright day with perfect conditions for sledding, but due to the bitter cold, there were very few people on the hill. They each rented a sled resembling a luge with a steering wheel. They exhausted themselves by racing most of the day. On their final run before going home, Johan flipped over. He went one way, and his sled went in the opposite direction. His helmet flew off, and he tumbled down the hill. Leah was behind him and watched in horror. She narrowly missed running into his sled with her own. She immediately stopped and ran to where he lay prone in the snow. She was already sobbing as she rolled him on his back, trying to be as gentle as possible. She didn't know if he might have sustained an injury, broken a bone, or worse.

"Johan!" she yelled. "Johan!"

She cradled his head and brushed the snow away from his face. He had a pained expression.

"Leah," he whispered. "My lovely Leah."

"Johan, where does it hurt? I'll go get help!"

"No, I'm—" His voice was faint.

"Oh my god, Johan! Don't you dare die on me!"

"Leah, I—"

"Yes, yes … I'm right here."

"I have something to ask you."

"What—what is it?"

"Will you marry me?"

Leah surmised he was delirious or had suffered a concussion. Distraught, she searched frantically to see if there was anyone she could call for help. She heard Johan moan, and then she saw the corners of his mouth turn upward slightly—it evolved into a grin. The mix of emotions made her cry even harder. She couldn't believe the audacity of him for joking with her in this way. She wanted to smack him for giving her the biggest fright of her life, but he grabbed her on top of him and squeezed her tight. They kissed until she lost feeling in her fingers and toes, but she didn't care—she could never resist his lips.

Leah hadn't thought of that day in so long and was upset with herself for getting emotional. She took a tissue out of her pocket and dabbed her cheeks before turning back toward Henrik's cabin. After taking only a few steps, she stopped dead in her tracks. Leah sensed two small, glimmering spheres fixated on her.

Something was blocking her path, but she couldn't make it out. Her tears and the blowing snow had blurred her vision. Panic-stricken, she blinked several times, and then she saw it. Her heart thumped uncontrollably. She didn't even dare take a breath.

Leah was staring into the glow of yellow pupils. It was a large tawny-colored cat with a ropelike tail that hung nearly to the ground. They were two beings running across each other in the night—each afraid to make the next move. She racked her brain to remember anything she had ever learned about encountering a wild animal. Was she supposed to run, make a lot of noise, or curl up and play dead? At that moment, she could barely remember her own name.

"Leah, stay perfectly still," said a voice. It was Henrik.

She had not heard him coming up behind her.

"Henrik, I … I—"

"Don't be afraid. I'm firing a shot." He spoke in a calm and concise manner.

She forced her eyes shut. It was only a few seconds later before Henrik pulled the trigger, but it felt like an eternity. When she heard the gunshot, her hair stood on end, and she fully expected to be pounced upon and mauled.

"You're safe now, Leah."

She realized Henrik now stood in front of her. She opened her eyes tentatively and squinted at him, still unable to focus.

"I … I don't know." She was in shock, and her ears were ringing.

"Come, you need to get inside." Henrik slung his rifle over his shoulder and wrapped his arm around her. She slumped against him for support, and they walked back to his cabin, not more than twenty feet from where they were.

"What would I have done without you?" She couldn't bring herself to think of it.

Henrik held her closer and propped her up. She heard the beating in his chest as she rested her head on him, half walking and half being dragged up the steps to his cabin.

Once inside, he carefully placed his rifle on a nearby table. He helped remove her coat and guided her in front of the roaring fireplace. Although Leah was not outside for long, her body felt frozen. She was happy to see the fire going, and the heat brought some comfort, though her heartbeat was still erratic.

Henrik handed her a glass of wine. He sat beside her and touched her knee. "You're safe now, Leah." He repeated the words she remembered him saying outside, as if to reassure her.

"Henrik, thank god you were there." She took a sip and saw her hand shaking. "What was that?"

"A cougar—a large male."

"A cougar?" She was stunned. She expected she might see coyotes here, but certainly nothing as rare as a mountain lion in this part of Canada.

She learned that Henrik had also heard the gunfire last night and suspected there might be an animal nearby. When she didn't show up, he went searching for her. She was so grateful he did.

"Was that your biathlon rifle?" she asked.

"Yes—a .22 caliber."

She found herself feeling remorseful. Was she responsible for having the cougar shot?

"Did you kill it?"

"No, I just scared it off. I would never kill an animal—certainly not one that magnificent."

"Thank goodness." She sighed, relieved. "I've never been so scared in my life."

"Leah, I'm sure he was more scared of you than you were of him."

"Somehow, I doubt that." She could tell he was making an effort to put her mind at ease, but she wasn't buying it. "Thank you, Henrik."

"For what?" He gazed at her in a way that made her weak.

"For saving my life."

"My pleasure."

Those deep chocolate-brown eyes and that mouth … She couldn't help herself. She cautiously leaned forward and kissed him, waiting for a sign from him to continue. If he seemed surprised, she didn't notice it. He reciprocated without hesitation. She could sense his muscular jaw as he licked her and twirled his tongue inside her. She welcomed his warmth, sucking on him and savoring the feel of his lips. At one point, he stopped and looked at her in a way that puzzled her.

"What?" She felt warm with vibrations.

"I've waited for someone like you, Leah."

His words frightened her. What did he mean? Suddenly, she saw Johan's face.

"Henrik …"

"Did I scare you?"

"I … I'm not sure. Maybe a little."

"No need to be," he said. He smiled and then changed the subject. "Are you hungry?"

Surprisingly, she was, although she didn't think she would be after her encounter with the cougar. "I'm famished."

"Good, let's eat, then. You need to regain your strength after that incident."

He was right. She already felt the effects from just a few sips of wine, and she didn't want to drink anymore until she got some food in her.

"Can I help you with anything?" she asked.

"No, I'm almost done. Make yourself at home. As you can see, the place looks very much like yours."

She decided to freshen up before dinner. He was right. The size of his cabin appeared similar to hers, with only a slightly different configuration. Despite that, she was intrigued being in his space and was curious to know more about him.

She had googled him. Henrik's bio stated he was born in Oslo, started out as an alpine skier, but switched to biathlon by the time he was sixteen. He had won numerous medals prior to the Olympics and was instrumental in improving the sport of biathlon. There was only one picture of him with his teammate at the Olympic medals ceremony from Salt Lake City. She remembered feeling a chill as she stared at his image. It was like seeing an old photograph of Johan.

Henrik was setting the table when she came out of the bathroom. He had taken off his sweater and was wearing a black T-shirt that hugged his chest, exposing his well-defined arms. He had the quintessential build of a biathlete—tall, lean, and muscular.

"Where did you learn to cook?" she asked.

"My mother. She said it was the best way to impress a woman."

She blushed, something she found herself doing a lot with him.

Henrik made a scrumptious meal of chicken and pasta tossed in olive oil with sun-dried tomatoes and olives. They also had a side salad of beets with toasted caraway seeds. Leah thoroughly enjoyed the food and the company. She was finally able to relax now that the angst from her cougar episode had faded.

After they finished dinner, she helped load the dishes before sitting on the couch with Henrik. He put another log on the fire. Leah had not forgotten his words, which hung between them like dense smoke. He was interested, that much she knew, but what did he mean when he said he had been waiting for someone like her? Was she reading too much into it?

"Leah, I have a confession to make." He looked at her seriously.

Her heart missed a beat. She thought if anyone should be confessing anything, it should be her. "What—what is it?"

"I came by your cabin earlier today."

"You did?" She didn't remember hearing anyone at her door. "Did you knock?"

"No, I heard loud music and just peered in your window. I didn't want to disturb you."

Leah wondered what he was talking about and then realized what she was doing at the time. She let out a giggle. "Oh! You came by and saw me boxing, didn't you?"

His impish grin gave it away. "Yes, it was quite a sight."

"You didn't want to join me?"

"Are you kidding? I've never seen that game before, but I felt sorry for your opponent!"

They both laughed. She was terrified he was going to drop something heavy on her, and it was a relief to have some levity between them.

"I must have looked ridiculous," she said.

"No, I wouldn't say that. On the contrary."

"Oh?"

"It was a sexy sight."

Henrik explained that he had come by to offer to escort her to his cabin that night but decided not to interrupt her.

It had been a long time since Leah was remotely interested in any man. She found herself shamelessly flirting with him. "You were aroused by watching me box?"

"Who wouldn't be?"

She blushed. "Maybe we should have a match. I have a second control you can use."

"No, I would never hit you!"

"Don't worry. It's only an avatar of me. It would be good to box against a real opponent, not just a computer-generated one." Leah took a deep breath and smelled the scent of burning firewood.

Henrik reached over and brushed a strand of hair that had fallen near her face. His fingers lingered, tracing a line down the side of her cheek.

She felt her insides dissolve as his touch sent pleasurable tremors throughout her body. There was no doubt she wanted him, but she wasn't ready to reconcile her feelings just yet. As attracted as she was to Henrik, she didn't want to treat him like all the other men she had dated since Johan's death. She had to know if he was the one she wanted—and not just because he reminded her so much of the only man she'd ever loved.

"Leah, lovely Leah," Henrik said.

Her eyes welled up immediately upon hearing those words. "I'm sorry … I have to go."

He looked confused. "Did I say something wrong?"

"No, no, you didn't, but it's late."

"Leah, please stay." He put his hand on her shoulder. "I'm not going to push you into anything. I'll drive you back if you want, but you know I have two extra bedrooms—you can use either one."

"I—"

"Remember, there's a wild cat out there." He gave her a knowing look.

She forced a smile. His invitation was genuine, and a big part of her was relieved she didn't have to go out in the cold again tonight.

*　　　　*　　　　*　　　　*

Leah was under the blankets in the room next to Henrik's. She could feel his presence through the wall. After she came to bed, she heard him moving about in the cabin, putting out the fire before going into his own room. She imagined him undressing and wondered what he looked like naked. A big part of her hoped he would just come into her room and take her, but she knew he wouldn't.

She lay awake for hours, burning with desire and aching for Henrik's touch. He had reawakened old feelings she thought she had long buried. More than once, she got out of bed with the intention of going into his room, but she changed her mind before reaching the door. She had to do something to alleviate her frustration.

Leah turned on the lamp next to her bed and saw that it was almost three in the morning. Her mind was racing and alive with ideas for her new book. She found a pen and paper and immediately started jotting down notes, not stopping until she had both sides of three sheets filled.

Meeting Henrik had somehow provided her with a germ of a story line that she liked. She was hopeful that this meant her wellspring of ideas was active and flowing again.

*　　　　*　　　　*　　　　*

Leah got up just before eight, but Henrik was nowhere to be seen. She found a note in the kitchen. It read:

Leah,
Help yourself to coffee.
I had a wonderful evening with you.
Henrik

The coffee was already brewed, and she poured a cup. She read the note again, picked up a pen, and added to it:

Me too,
Leah

She kept her response brief, and she didn't want to assume too much. His words gave no indication of when he would return or whether he wanted to see her again. She experienced a sinking feeling in her stomach that perhaps she had blown her chances with him.

When Leah had finally fallen asleep, she had numerous dreams. The only one she recalled had a cougar running toward her, but for some reason, she was unafraid. Just as the large cat was about to pounce, the image changed to her falling into Henrik's arms. Not one to normally remember her dreams, she was amazed at how vividly this one stuck in her mind.

It was the morning of Christmas Eve, and Leah walked back to her cabin after she finished the coffee. She was grateful Henrik had invited her to stay over. Part of her didn't want to admit she was nervous about being alone in the evenings.

After taking a hot shower and eating breakfast, she sat on the couch with her computer. The sun was streaming into her cabin, and outside her window, she saw huge evergreens, their branches laden with snow that had fallen during the past few days. Some of it was already melting.

Leah sent Christmas wishes to friends and family and responded to e-mails. She also sent a note to her mother about Henrik with a link to the picture of him. She had resolved to scrap everything she wrote previously and start fresh on her new book. She was anxious to type what she'd written down last night, uncertain whether ideas would come as freely as they had prior to her writer's block. For the time being, though, she would settle for her inspiration in spurts as long as there wasn't another dry spell.

Leah did not stop typing until midafternoon. She didn't even break for lunch, choosing instead to snack on carrot sticks and cheese and crackers. It felt like a thick fog had finally lifted, and she was able to think clearly again. After rereading her words, she was pleased with how the story was developing and concluded it had been a productive day. She was just about to shut down when she heard the *ding* of an incoming e-mail. It was from her mother. She was curious to see what she had to say about Henrik. Her note read:

Hi, Leah,

It's great to hear you have found some inspiration for your next book. That's excellent news!

I'm even happier you have met Henrik and are not alone for the holidays. I looked at the link you attached of

him. Leah, I must disagree with you—I don't really see a
resemblance to Johan.

I may never have told you this, but after your dad died, I
saw his face in every man I met. That is, until your stepfather
came along, and I realized I had to see him with different
eyes.

The similarities Henrik shares with Johan are that they
are both Norwegian, have the same first name, and are
athletic. Aside from this, they are two very different men who
happen to have certain qualities—ones you are obviously
attracted to. You've focused on the similarities, but you know
there are differences—you just need to see them. If you still
like him after that, I think you should pursue the relationship.

I know how much you loved Johan. It was a tragedy
he died so young, but you are still a young woman yourself.
You need to trust that someone else can make you happy. You
certainly deserve it. It's your time, my dear.

Be sure to eat a nice Christmas dinner.
Love,
Mom

After reading the e-mail twice, Leah turned off the computer. She was surprised to feel tears dampen her cheeks.

She had enormous respect for her mother's opinion. A child psychologist and accomplished author herself, she had always been Leah's role model, and they were extremely close. When Leah was only thirteen, her father died of a heart attack. After being alone for five years, her mother remarried.

Leah wanted to take her advice, but she was shocked her mother couldn't see the resemblance. As far as she was concerned, Henrik could have easily passed for Johan's twin. She decided not to think about it, as she wasn't sure where things stood after last night anyway. Just then, she heard a knock on the door.

Leah wiped her face and went to answer it. She had to snicker when she saw Henrik standing there wearing a pair of shorts, a T-shirt, and red boxing gloves.

"You must be frozen!" she screamed.

"I would have been if you didn't answer the door!" he said as he jumped inside.

"Why are you in that getup?"

He looked incredible, despite the ridiculous-looking gloves.

"I thought about the Wii boxing game after our conversation, and I may have dismissed it prematurely." He took off the gloves.

She had to chuckle, trying not to appear too obvious at how happy she was to see him.

"You want to incorporate Wii boxing into your training?" she asked.

"Why not? It would certainly be different, and it's important for athletes to have variety."

"All right, then, we must have a match so you can test it out."

"My thinking, exactly." He took a step closer to her. "That is—if you're up for it."

"Oh, I am," she said, attempting to intimidate him with her stare. Even though Henrik caught her by surprise, Leah never passed up a challenge.

It was the first chance she had to see him in the daylight, and she noticed that his eyes were not the dark chocolate color she had initially thought. They were actually hazel with green flecks. She felt hypnotized by them for a moment and remembered her mother's words: *There are differences—you just need to see them.*

Leah changed into a different sports bra from the one she'd worn yesterday and put on a pair of shorts. As an afterthought, she also threw on a T-shirt, not wanting to appear overtly flirtatious.

She showed Henrik how to operate the controls and decided to leave the sound of the game on so he could experience the full effects of it. They both created avatars that best represented themselves and started the first match. One game consisted of three individual rounds, each one lasting three minutes.

Leah won the first match as Henrik familiarized himself with how to use the Nunchuk. She knocked him out after the second round and did an enthusiastic victory dance in front of him. Leah was not a gracious winner.

"Thank you, thank you very much!" she said to the simulated cheers of the crowd in the game.

"Okay, no more chances for you, Leah," Henrik said. "I was just warming up."

They boxed energetically for a half hour, huffing, puffing, and cursing.

"Take that!" she yelled as she knocked out Henrik's avatar with an uppercut. The countdown began—one, two, three—but he got up, and they were at it again. At one point, Henrik got so carried away and punched the air with such force his remote flew out of his hand and struck the television. Leah was almost afraid he had cracked the screen. She cackled hysterically at how absurd the game was, but neither of them wanted to stop. Another fifteen minutes later, they were drenched and had shed their T-shirts.

Leah couldn't help but notice Henrik's sculpted chest and stomach. He was in excellent shape. Seeing the muscles in his arms and legs had already aroused her, but now she was even more distracted. Physically and mentally drained, she could no longer focus on the game. That's when Henrik knocked her out.

"You're staying down!" he shouted at her avatar, and she did. It was an hour of intense cardio exercise for her, and it appeared he had gotten a good workout too.

"I give!" she said. "You win!"

She gasped for air and doubled over, laughing with her hands on her waist, trying to catch her breath. On a blissful high from the adrenaline rush, she straightened up to see him glaring at her. No words were needed. He dropped his Nunchuk and grabbed her, kissing her with such passion she just about lost consciousness. She yielded to him, feeling his heat as her breasts crushed up against him. Unable to control their balance, they fell backward onto the couch, locking lips and limbs.

Leah sat on top of him, and they kissed for a long time. When she touched his chest, she felt an electric shock go through her. His bare skin was glistening with sweat. She dismounted him and saw the bulge through his bike shorts—she had to have him.

Leah sank to her knees in front of Henrik and looked up to see him eyeing her with lust. She knew he wanted her. Leah tugged his shorts off, and his penis bounced out and almost slapped her in the face. She immediately blushed when she laid eyes on how spectacular he was.

His erection stood up hard and shiny. Surrounded by tight curls of pubic hair, he was big, not only in length, but also in girth. Leah felt a quiver down her spine just from the sight of him. All she thought of was how he could fill her up.

She stroked him lightly before enclosing his rod in her hand with a firm squeeze. A liquid bead protruded from the eye of his silky tip. She lapped up the wetness, and he squirmed in his seat. Relaxing her grip slightly, she flicked the rim.

Henrik threaded his fingers through her hair and dropped his head back. Leah teased him, offering him tiny kisses across the full length of him. Fluttering and swirling around his sensitive ridge, Leah made sure no part of him escaped her fiery tongue. She immersed herself deeper to lick and caress his balls. She reached up to pinch his nipples until they stood up erect. When she heard him groan, she clawed down his abdomen.

Henrik sighed and pushed himself toward her. She could tell he was incredibly excited and wanted her to inhale him. Grasping him, she enclosed her mouth over his glans, maintaining a strong hold of him as she moved deliberately along his shaft—leisurely withdrawing on the upstroke and quickly on the downstroke. She did this repeatedly, taking him deeper inside each time.

"Leah, my god … my god …" He was incomprehensible.

She swallowed continuously with his cock lodged in her throat until she felt him let go of her hair. She clutched his ass and knew he was close to coming. His entire body stiffened before the tremors rippled through him.

Henrik grunted and unloaded into her. He shook so powerfully that he almost slipped out, but she wouldn't let him. She held him tightly and felt the muscles of his buttocks clench while he squirted. She milked him, gulping his hot cum until he was depleted. When he finally stopped jerking, she licked around his scrotum to make sure she didn't miss a drop.

Leah got up off the floor and straddled him. His eyes were still shut when she nuzzled him behind his ear. It took him some time to get his breathing restored to normal.

"I may never walk again," he said, letting out a big sigh.

She smiled at him. "Does that mean you don't want a rematch?"

"Leah, you've ruined me for that. I can't even feel my legs."

She giggled and moved to kiss him on the forehead, noticing a scar above his right brow. It looked like an old wound. She outlined it with her finger. "How did you get this?"

"Hockey stick. I got hit when I was eight."

She leaned forward and kissed the scar. "I like it," she said. "It's you, and it's unique."

Henrik held her chin and touched his lips to hers. He was tender, but she sensed his need for her. Leah cuddled up to him. She had not felt this way in so long and was not sure whether she had ever had these feelings. With that realization came immediate sadness mixed with pain—the pain of letting go. She would always keep Johan's memory alive, but there was an emptiness in her life since he'd died. Was she ready to have that space filled? And was Henrik the man to do it?

She moved away from him. Her mother was right. She was starting to see the differences.

"Leah, are you all right?" he asked.

"Yes … I am." She choked back tears. "I'm just happy you're here, Henrik."

"Me too." He tapped her playfully on the nose. "Do you know what time it is?"

"No."

"It's Christmas." His watch showed five o'clock.

She had a vague recollection that all the church bells rang at five in Norway on Christmas Eve.

"Merry Christmas, Leah." He kissed her again. "I would like to invite you out for dinner tonight."

"Christmas dinner?"

"Yes."

The last Christmas dinner she'd had was with Johan's family in Bergen. She remembered a traditional feast of cod, pork, and a special dark beer that was available only for the holidays. It was a fond memory, and she had to admit she'd missed it over the last four years.

"Where are we going?" she asked.

"To visit some friends of mine, he said. "You'll like them."

"Uh … are you sure it's okay that I come with you?"

"Yes, of course. You'll enjoy yourself. I promise."

She quickly realized she still had nothing to wear.

"I like what you have on now," he said, drawing her close to nuzzle her neck.

"I'm serious." She pushed him away halfheartedly.

Henrik reassured her it was casual, and they would find another occasion where they could dress up. His words implied a future for them, something she had not seen with anyone else since Johan's death.

*   *   *   *

After Henrik left, Leah spent a half hour in the hot tub to relax her tired muscles. It was a bitterly cold evening and the first night since she'd arrived that it was not snowing. For dinner, she wore a black wool skirt and a black lace camisole under a pale green cardigan. She applied a little makeup and just a dab of perfume—Lovely, her favorite scent.

Henrik arrived promptly at seven o'clock to pick her up. He looked incredible with a gray turtleneck sweater, black jacket, and a pair of black jeans. When he hugged her, she wallowed in the essence of his raw masculinity.

They drove a short distance from Cedar Valley to a town called Huntsville. She was not familiar with the area, which was a residential neighborhood. Moments later, they pulled into the driveway of a large house. There were strings of white lights adorning the shrubbery at the entrance, and she saw a fully decorated Christmas tree behind the bay windows. They got out of the car and proceeded up the freshly shoveled walkway.

Henrik rang the doorbell, and a woman answered. An attractive brunette in her forties, she gave them a big grin.

"Henrik, my dear," she said.

"Hi, Norah."

"Please come in. It's freezing outside."

They entered the house, and Henrik gave Norah a big hug before introducing her. "Norah, this is Leah."

The two women exchanged pecks on both cheeks. Henrik shook hands with a man who came up behind Norah and gave him the bottle of wine and chocolates they'd brought. He was Norah's husband, Michael Simms—coach of the National Canadian biathlon team. Michael was a tall, pleasant-looking man in his midforties, and he'd been the coach for the past couple of seasons. It was his idea to bring Henrik in to improve the training program for his team.

They sat in the living room drinking mulled apple cider as Christmas carols played in the background. The tree Leah had seen from the outside of the house was spectacular. She recognized it as a Fraser fir from its sweet fragrance and silvery green needles. She had forgotten all the fabulous sights, sounds, and smells of Christmas, and felt a bit homesick for the celebrations she used to have with her own family.

"Leah, would you like to help me in the kitchen?" Norah asked.

"Of course." She glanced over to Henrik, who gave her a wink before she left the room.

Norah and Michael had three teenage children and lived in a grand house, beautifully decorated with pictures of family on many of the walls. There were also numerous plaques and awards in Michael's name. He had been part of the Canadian biathlon team before becoming its coach.

Norah offered Leah a glass of wine and poured one for herself as well.

"You have a beautiful home," Leah said. "It's so cozy and inviting."

"Thank you. When you have kids, it's a revolving door for all their friends too, so we've tried to make it as comfortable as possible."

"You've done a great job."

"Thanks," Norah said and then paused. "Leah, may I make an observation?"

"Yes, of course."

"I must say I haven't seen Henrik so happy in a long time. He's smitten with you."

Her remark caught Leah totally off guard. "He's a very special person," she finally said.

"Yes, he is. He and Michael met almost a decade ago on the circuit and have been friends ever since. We've stayed with him in Oslo while on vacation." She handed a casserole of green beans to Leah.

"These smell fantastic," she said, setting the dish on the dining room table. She noticed there were only four place settings. "Will your children not be joining us?"

"No, we have our family dinner tomorrow night. They're with friends, happy to get away from us for a few hours during the holidays."

They both laughed and made some small talk about rebellious teens.

"Henrik mentioned you're a writer."

"Yes, I am."

"His last girlfriend was also a writer. You remind me of her."

"Oh? In what way?"

"Similar energy—that ethereal quality—and, of course, the physical beauty as well."

"That's kind of you to say. Does Henrik still keep in touch with her?"

Norah's expression immediately changed, and she appeared sullen. "I'm sorry, Leah ... I was assuming you already knew."

"Knew—knew about what?"

Norah looked very uncomfortable. "My apologies. I've spoken out of turn."

"I see." For some reason, Leah felt as if *she* needed to diffuse the awkward situation, even though she had not created it. "No harm done ... really, Norah. I don't want you to feel like you're betraying Henrik's confidence."

"Thank you." Norah seemed relieved. "I forget that Henrik is a private person sometimes, but I thought ... I just think it's best if Henrik tells you about her," she said, adding, "I'm sure he will."

"Of course. Henrik and I haven't had many opportunities to talk at length."

"I appreciate your understanding," Norah said sheepishly.

Leah couldn't help asking her one more question, though. "Can you just tell me when the relationship ended?"

"Uh ... I guess that would be okay. It was right after Henrik won his silver medal."

Leah's heart sank. It was not a good sign that it was over eight years ago.

All along, she'd questioned her own feelings for Henrik ... and whether they were genuine. Now that she was beginning to like him for who he was, it appeared he had also been comparing her to someone from his past. She found herself wondering about his ex-girlfriend. What was she like? Did she break his heart? Was he still pining for her?

Leah tried to push aside her concerns about Henrik when they sat down to eat. She felt fortunate to have dinner with him and his friends on Christmas Eve. Michael and Norah were gracious hosts and went out of their way to make her feel welcome. It was obvious they cared a great deal about Henrik.

She didn't want to overdo it with the savory rack of lamb, but it was so succulent that she had to have a second helping. During coffee and trifle for dessert, she sensed Henrik's fingers brush her knee under the table. He had been attentive to her all evening. She really wanted to believe she had found another chance at love.

*　　*　　*　　*

It was snowing again as Henrik pulled up to her cabin. He built a fire and joined her on the couch.

Leah's conversation with Norah crept back into her consciousness, and she knew she needed to talk to Henrik about it. She wasn't sure how to bring up his past and thought it best to share about herself, hoping that would start the conversation.

"I had a wonderful time tonight, Henrik. Thank you."

"I'm glad you enjoyed it. Mike and Norah are salt of the earth."

"Yes, they are lovely people, and I can see how fond they are of you."

He sat next to her, holding her hand and stroking her hair. "You're so beautiful, Leah," he said, leaning in for a kiss.

She felt his tongue tickle her lips and send pleasurable chills straight to her pussy. Henrik turned her on as no man ever had. He was patient, a quality neither she nor Johan possessed when they were with each other.

As much as she wanted to get lost in Henrik's touch, she reluctantly moved away from him. "Henrik."

"Yes, my darling Leah."

She loved how he said her name.

"I want to tell you a little bit about myself."

"All right," he said. "I want to know everything about you."

She offered a weak smile. "This … this is difficult." Leah took a deep breath and fought to keep her emotions from taking hold of her.

Henrik cupped her hands in his. "Leah, trust me. You can tell me anything." It was as if he were giving her permission to disclose a secret.

"All right …" She felt heat rise to her cheeks. "H. J. Carlsen is … *was* … the name of my fiancé. He went by his middle name—Johan—but his given name was also Henrik." She saw his expression change slightly, but he didn't interrupt her. "That's why I was so shocked when you showed up at my door … Johan died four years ago—weeks before we were to be married."

"I'm so sorry, Leah."

"The truth is, you looked so much like him, or … how he would have looked if he were still alive." Leah fought the urge to get emotional.

"Leah—"

"No, please, Henrik, let me finish. It's been so long since I've wanted to be with anyone. Since Johan died, I've compared all men to him, and I felt like I was doing the same thing with you. Everything about you reminded me of him, until—"

"Until?"

"Until I began seeing you through different eyes. There are obvious similarities, but there are also differences—I had just chosen to ignore them." Leah was surprised by her admission. Verbalizing it made it real for her. "Henrik, I know so little about you. All I know is how I feel when I'm with you."

He gazed at her with affection. "Leah, may I ask you a question?"

She hesitated, not realizing she was crying until he wiped her tears. "Yes."

"How did Johan die?"

"An accident. He was ski-BASE jumping off the Eiger, and his parachute malfunctioned—it never opened."

"That's tragic."

There was silence between them for a moment. Leah wasn't sure what else to say. Henrik had listened intently, but now she was aware of her vulnerability.

"Leah, do you remember when you came by for dinner? And I told you I've waited for someone like you?"

"Uh-huh," she whispered. How could she forget?

"I didn't mean to say it like that. I know it caught you off guard."

"You're right ... it did." She took a deep breath. What was he trying to tell her?

"I must apologize, Leah, as what I meant to say was ..."

She didn't listen to anything else after that. She could smell a setup for an explanation she had already played out in her head, and she couldn't bear to hear how she didn't measure up to his last girlfriend.

"Henrik, it's okay. You don't need to explain." She moved to get off the couch, knowing she couldn't look at him anymore or she would start crying again.

"Leah—"

"No, no, Henrik, I don't want to hear it, and you certainly don't owe me a thing—"

"Leah, please—"

She stood up, feeling sick to her stomach and wanting to kick herself for being honest with him. "I can't—I don't want to hear how I'm not the one you want."

"Leah, listen to me!" Henrik got up and held her tear-stained face. "You *are* the one I want. I haven't allowed myself to get close to anyone—last night with you was ..."

"What?"

"It was the first time I've felt anything in a long time."

"I ... I don't follow." She searched his face for answers, but all she saw was despair.

"Like you, I also lost someone I loved ... only it wasn't an accident." He sat back on the couch and took her hand.

After a moment, she joined him.

"Her name was Finna," he said. "She committed suicide, and I blamed myself for what happened. It's the real reason I retired from biathlon—I no longer had the desire for the sport, nor the will to compete."

She felt devastated for him.

He told her about Finna, a screenwriter from Norway. They were together for almost seven years. During their relationship, she developed a screenplay about the life of Norwegian jazz singer Radka Toneff, who took her own life at the age of thirty. Finna tried to sell the script, but she had no success. Henrik's achievements, on the other hand, continued to mount. When he was accepted on the Olympics team, Finna was already having problems with depression. He promised to spend more time with her once the games were over. Soon after he returned home, Finna killed herself. She was twenty-nine.

When Henrik finished his story, Leah wasn't sure how she could console him or whether he even wanted her to.

"Henrik, you can't blame yourself for Finna's suicide. It wasn't your fault."

"I know, but I was selfish, thinking only about myself."

"No, Henrik, you weren't selfish. You were an athlete, and training and competition were part of your life."

"Perhaps, but I guess Finna wanted a different life. She felt neglected, and she just couldn't wait for me any longer." Henrik spoke with real sadness in his voice.

"I understand," she said. "I really do." She explained about Johan's daredevil nature, and how he had sought increasingly dangerous activities while they were together. They were young and thought they would live forever. Even though they both knew the risks, she never once cautioned him against making any of his jumps. After he died, she wondered if she should have prevented him from pursuing such a deadly sport. She also went through an anger period, blaming Johan for instigating his own demise. "You see, Henrik, I thought he had been selfish in not taking better care of himself, in destroying our chance for a life together."

"Do you still feel that way?"

"No, I realized what he did and who he was were inextricable. His adventurous spirit was what made me fall in love with him. It would have been selfish of *me* to ask him to change because I was afraid to lose him."

She wrung her hands, averting Henrik's eyes. She didn't want him to think she was implying Finna had been the selfish one.

"Leah, you're an incredible woman." He looked at her with tenderness.

"Oh, Henrik, I don't know about that." She couldn't fathom how heartbreaking it must have been to lose someone to suicide.

"Are you still grieving for Johan?"

"No, no, of course not. He's gone now. I'm over it." Leah was stunned to hear how flippant she sounded about Johan's death. It made her take pause and wonder, and then she felt tightness in her throat and was unable to breathe. She swallowed a gasp and started coughing.

It suddenly hit her that she had never really mourned Johan—not in the traditional sense. Of course, she had attended the funeral service and was there for the burial, but he was still very much alive in her. Taking his identity right after he died meant he continued to live in her stories. It had helped her to cope, but it had also inhibited her—she had never let go. With that revelation, she began to weep.

*   *   *   *

Leah woke up to find herself lying on the couch covered in a blanket. The fire had long burnt out, and light was flooding into the room. The clock on the wall showed seven thirty. She sat up but didn't see Henrik. The memories of the previous evening slowly invaded her consciousness. She recalled crying in Henrik's arms and realized she must have collapsed from exhaustion.

It had been a difficult night for both of them, and she had experienced an epiphany of sorts. Her catharsis, however, wiped her out emotionally and physically. How was she going to face Henrik after her breakdown? Just then, she heard footsteps approaching her cabin.

Henrik came in dressed in full skin-tight biathlon gear. A gust of wind picked up the snow behind him and blew it inside before he was able to close the door.

"Good morning, Leah."

She rubbed the sleep from her eyes and saw how incredibly sexy he looked. "Henrik, where have you been?"

He had been up since six, skiing and shooting targets. He had on a one-piece black Lycra racing suit, goggles on top of his head, and his rifle strapped to his back. His suit left little to the imagination. She couldn't help but stare at his muscular ripples, nor could she avoid sneaking a peek at the bulge between his legs. Walking toward her, he resembled an artic hunter, and she swore she could even feel the chill off his body.

He sat next to her and gave her a kiss. His lips felt cool.

"Henrik, about last night …"

"Leah, let's have some fun today." He touched her cheek, tracing the stains of her tears.

Fun? That was unexpected.

"Uh … okay," she said. "What did you have in mind?"

"How would you like to go tobogganing?"

"Tobogganing?" She had not done that since the day Johan proposed.

"Yes, you know, you take a sled and—"

"I know what it is," she said—a tad sharply. She immediately softened her tone. "Okay … I need some fun."

Henrik didn't seem to notice her uneasiness. "The hills should be pretty quiet." He reached out and held her hands. "I'd like to spend my last day here with you, Leah."

She'd forgotten he was leaving. In their short time together, Henrik had stirred up the full spectrum of emotions in her. She was sure he felt the same way. She couldn't blame him for wanting to end things off with her on a lighter note.

Leah no longer had doubts about him. Coincidences and similarities aside, she wanted him. It seemed so unfair that she would only come to this realization on the day before he was leaving.

*   *   *   *

They walked to a steep, rolling hill not far from Cedar Valley. The overnight snowfall had deposited a fresh blanket of white on the ground. Overall, there was nearly two feet of it.

Henrik was right; there was no one there. It was too cold and too early. She guessed most people were still at home with family, opening presents like she used to as a kid on Christmas morning.

Henrik secured a couple of "flying saucers" from the resort. They were quite different from the high-tech sleds Leah had used with Johan. On the slippery plastic disc with only two rope handles to cling to, Leah screamed for dear life as she sailed down the steep hills, spinning uncontrollably with little hope of steering.

They had numerous races, and on some of them, she slid backward all the way, picked up speed, hit a bump, and flew off. It was probably the most dangerous sled she had ever been on, but it was also the most fun she had experienced in ages. At one point, she was in stitches and thought she might actually pee in her snow pants from laughing so hard. They were at it for almost two hours before she realized how wet she was.

"Okay," she said, out of breath, approaching the top of the hill where Henrik was waiting for her. "This is it for me." Leah was exhausted and could barely stand up on her rubbery legs.

"All right, just one more race," Henrik said.

"Okay, last one."

"Deal. Let's make it a good one."

"I'm ready," she said, positioning herself as securely as possible on the wobbly saucer.

"How about we make it more interesting by placing a wager?"

She clapped her gloves together, eager for the challenge. "What would you suggest?"

"A massage—I sure could use one."

She giggled. "You're so certain *you* will win?"

"It's a forgone conclusion."

"I'll have to prove you wrong, then, won't I?" His cockiness only made her more determined to beat him. "Okay, on a count of three," she said, holding on tightly to the ropes.

"One …" She fixed her eyes on the path in front of her. "Two … Three!" Leah pushed off and descended the hill. She had a slight lead and was gaining speed, but so was he. Henrik's weight worked in his favor, and she knew he would propel by her if she didn't change her course. Leah saw the only way she could win. She swerved into Henrik's path, clipping his sled ever so slightly. He fell off balance for a second, but that was all she required to glide past him. As long as she didn't spin out of control now, she would be able to finish ahead of him, which she did.

"What was that?" he yelled, as he came to a stop behind her at the bottom of the hill.

"That was a little maneuver to help me win!"

They were both panting from exhaustion and soaked through and through.

"You deserve to be disqualified," he said.

"I don't remember seeing any rules and regulations prior to the race!" she scoffed.

Leah fell on the powdery snow and made a snow angel, something she hadn't done since she was a kid. She gazed into the cloudless blue sky, drawing the crisp air into her lungs. Off in the distance, she heard the laughter of children. She did miss having fun, and she hadn't allowed herself much of it since Johan died.

Her view of the sky was suddenly obstructed by Henrik's face. He had taken off his goggles and helmet and was looking at her with those hazel eyes. He bent to kiss her with his cold lips, and she pulled him on top of her. Even in her damp suit, she felt the warmth from their embrace course through her body. They lay in the snow, basking in the sun's rays. It was only when a child on a wooden toboggan slid beside them that they realized there were now more people on the hill.

They planned their day on the way back to her cabin—brunch at his place and dinner at hers. In between, they had to fit in her massage and find time for the hot tub, a sauna, and anything else they could think of. It was as if they wanted to live the rest of their lives in the next twenty-four hours.

*   *   *   *

She arrived at Henrik's just as he was setting the table. As always, he looked incredible. Not since Johan had she met anyone who exuded so much confidence and charisma. He wore a light cotton shirt and jeans, and his hair was still damp. When Leah sat next to him, she smelled the faint fragrance from his shampoo, and it made her weak.

He'd made a nutritious brunch of egg and cheese on English muffins, fruit, and fresh orange juice. They were both ravenous after expending their energy outside for hours.

"That was the most fun I've had in … I can't even remember when," she said, biting into her sandwich. "Thank you."

"Me too. I think we both needed it."

"Yes … When is your flight tomorrow?"

"Noon. I'll have to get an early start—I have to return the rental car too."

She wished he wasn't leaving. "Do you know what you'll do when you get back?"

"I have a few options. I've had several offers for coaching jobs, but I'm not sure that's where my heart is right now."

"Where is it, then?"

He wiped his mouth with a napkin and looked seriously at her. "I found something very important when I met you, Leah … something I thought I had lost."

"What's that?" She held her breath.

"Desire."

She exhaled and felt heat rise to her face. "You mean to compete again?"

"Yes, that had crossed my mind, but more importantly, desire to share my life with someone. I've been numb for so long, but I feel alive again, and … and I owe it all to you, Leah." There was no trace of sadness in his voice.

She blushed. "Henrik, thank you for the compliment, but I can't take the credit."

"I'm not trying to flatter you. It's the truth. You're the best Christmas present I never expected."

She loved the poetic symbolism because she felt the same about him. "You've given me a lot too."

"Really?"

"Yes, I'm able to write again."

Henrik seemed thrilled. "That's fantastic. You have a story line for your book now?"

"I'm still working out the plot, but it's moving along quite nicely. It's about a biathlete."

He smiled and raised his eyebrows. "Tell me more."

Leah never discussed her stories with anyone except her editor, but she was willing to make an exception for Henrik. "He's the perfect male specimen, with unparalleled stamina and precision marksmanship. He's been hired by the Canadian government to find a woman who's been kidnapped while on vacation skiing in Norway."

Henrik grinned from ear to ear as she told him about her story. "Hmm, that sounds vaguely familiar. Maybe she's been abducted by a large mountain lion."

"Maybe."

"Or maybe she's been kidnapped by the very man they've hired to find her."

Leah cozied up to Henrik. "You're giving me ideas," she said. "What else do you see happening?"

"Maybe she doesn't want to be found."

"Go on."

"She doesn't want to go back to Canada."

"And why not?"

"She wants to be with the man who stole her heart."

Leah felt a lump in her throat. "You're good."

The sexual tension between them was incredible. She was already wet with desire halfway through their meal. Leah would have been happy for him to take her right there at the table. When Henrik kissed her, she melted into him and clawed at his chest to undo his shirt. Primal instinct took over, and all she could think of was how much she wanted to touch his bare skin.

Henrik stood up, taking her with him, and swept her into his arms. Leah snuggled against him as he carried her to his bedroom, nibbling his neck all the while. She recalled the night she'd stayed in the room beside his, imagining what it would feel like to be with him, and now here she was.

Like her bedroom at the Raven, he had a king-sized bed. He placed her on it and sat next to her. Leah was shaking with need as she watched him undress her. She wanted to help him, but she was paralyzed by his touch, totally engrossed in how he made her feel. She was desperate to be possessed by him. He left her clad only in her black bra and panties.

"My god Leah," he said. "You're so lovely."

She heard his words as if she were hearing them for the first time.

He got up and started undoing his shirt, which she had already half unbuttoned. After taking off his pants and underwear, he stood naked in front of her.

Leah knelt on the bed and stared at his erection. It was pointing directly at her, beckoning for her touch. She remembered the taste of him and couldn't resist indulging herself again. She took hold of his cock and stroked him until he groaned her name.

"Leah ..."

She enclosed just the knob in her mouth and gave him quick jabs with her tongue. She formed a vacuum-like seal around him and moved her head in a circular motion across the entire shaft. She sucked him hard as she withdrew and heard a popping sound each time the head slid past her lips. Leah cupped his balls and caressed them when she felt his fingers grasp her hair, stopping her from going any further.

He got on the bed, kissing her with violent passion as his body covered hers. She couldn't breathe, but she didn't care. Her need for him eclipsed everything—growing to the point where she dug her nails into his butt until he shuddered. He left her lips and traveled across to her neck, nibbling, biting, and descending the curves of her body.

He kneaded her breasts through the fabric of her bra before sliding the straps off her shoulders. She arched her back as he reached behind her to free her mounds. She felt his hunger for her. "Henrik, please ..." She was on fire.

He was in no hurry. "Leah," he said, prolonging her torment, "I'm going to make love to you all day."

"Oh, yes ..."

"And after I'm done, I'm making love to you all night—you won't soon forget the stamina of a biathlete."

"Ohhh ..." She was trembling as she pushed herself toward him, silently pleading with him to touch her. She knew he wouldn't be able to resist her for much longer.

Henrik dove into her cleavage. He fondled her tits before licking each one, taking her nipples into his mouth to flick them until they both became engorged. Every time he brushed his hard tongue against her twin peaks, she quivered in response.

She raised both arms above her head, crossing them at the wrists as he continued to ravage her, trailing downward with his lips.

Henrik was between her legs and had slid off her panties. There would be no hiding how excited she was. She was neatly trimmed and glistening with desire. She heard him gulp when he saw her exposed to him. He rested his chin in front of her pussy. She drew her knees up and felt him rub her juices over her labia before inserting two fingers into her. Her snatch enveloped him in its smooth, snug walls and didn't want to let go.

"My god, Leah, you're so wet."

He plummeted his tongue into her twat, merciless as he jabbed her hole. He grabbed her ass to lift her closer to him. One moment, he was loudly lapping her—and then he was slowly tickling her until she cried out for more.

When Leah's moans grew louder, he sucked on her clit. The feeling was so overpowering that she almost passed out. Dizzy with lust, she felt Henrik stab her nub. A thunderous explosion rippled up her stomach, and she released a growl that sounded possessed. She went into multiple spasms, soaking the sheets with her sticky fluid.

Henrik gently kissed along her swollen slit and lingered between her inner thighs. His face was shiny with her cum. When he made his way up to her again, she smelled her scent on him.

Leah sensed Henrik's hardness between them. He had gotten more aroused after eating her. He took out a condom and ripped it open. She knew, without a doubt, that he ached for her as much as she did for him.

She could not wait to feel him inside her. "Henrik, I want you so much ... I—"

He plunged into her with ruthless passion. In one stroke, he filled her up to the hilt. No man had ever penetrated her so deeply. Flexing her ass muscles, she squeezed his shaft and locked her legs around his waist.

Leah's feverish writhing spurred him on until he was moving like a piston in a well-lubricated cylinder. She felt every inch of him as he injected himself into her, and when he pulled out, he grazed her delicate entrance with his knob before he pounded her again. He fucked her savagely.

She gasped for air, and her body begged for relief. When she felt tremors coursing through her, she raked her nails across Henrik's back. Leah screamed as she came again, clenching Henrik's cock as the swells of her orgasm singed every fiber of her being.

He got up on his knees and held both her legs together by the ankles. Leah was almost vertical as he kissed and nibbled her feet. He took one final lunge.

She saw Henrik close his eyes in pleasurable agony. He let out a guttural sound and jerked several times. He came, beads of sweat slick on his skin. She expected him to collapse, but he didn't—he continued prodding her. She soon realized he was not ready to stop. He was a machine.

With tremendous strength and agility, he pivoted her on top of him. He lay on his back, propped up by his forearms. Leah straddled him with his cock firmly embedded in her.

"Leah, you're killing me," he said. "But I can't get enough of you."

His gluttony fueled her own. She rocked her hips, and he grew harder. Leah bent forward and he pushed her breasts together, alternating his tongue from one nipple to the other. She nuzzled his neck and bit his earlobes.

Leah held on to his shoulders, thrusting herself up and down to ride him. She bounced and reached behind her to tickle his balls.

When Leah came again, it was like a tiny spark that erupted into an inferno in seconds. Henrik held her ass tightly against his groin throughout her convulsions. As she came, she felt a gush of semen scorch her pussy. She crumpled on top of him as he finally surrendered to a lengthy, blissful climax.

*   *   *   *

Leah woke up disoriented from their afternoon lovemaking session. She forgot where she was until she turned to find Henrik beside her. He was on his stomach, and his arm was draped over her. She took a moment to watch him sleep. He snored lightly, unlike the sounds of the wild man she'd experienced only an hour earlier. Though she had suspected he would make a good lover, his voracious appetite nonetheless astounded her.

She slid out of bed and walked to the window. The sun would be setting soon. For some reason, that created an urgency in her to wake Henrik up.

When she approached him, though, she didn't have the heart to do it. He looked too peaceful.

Leah tiptoed out of the bedroom. She passed the dining room and saw all the dishes and leftover food still on the table from their brunch. She thought about the flirtatious episode that started it all and felt her mouth go dry. She grabbed some leftover orange juice and downed it.

Henrik's bathroom was identical to hers, equipped with a large stall and a showerhead with multiple settings. She picked up a few of his toiletries and saw that they had Norwegian writing on them. She recognized the lettering from the language course she had taken years ago. It brought back bittersweet memories of Johan.

Leah entered the shower, closed the glass door, and turned on the taps. She adjusted the water temperature until it was almost scalding. The heat of the pulsating jets felt incredible pounding her sore muscles. She glanced at her breasts and couldn't believe how dark her nipples were. Henrik had really ravaged them.

She shampooed her hair and squirted liquid soap in her palm. When she touched her mound, she was amazed at how swollen and hypersensitive she was. She closed her eyes, daydreaming as she caressed herself, remembering Henrik's fingers, his mouth, his cock …

"I'm the one who should be doing that," he said, sliding open the door to join her.

"Henrik, you startled me!" Leah instinctively pulled her hand away from her crotch.

"I'm sorry, but please don't stop. I like seeing you enjoy yourself," he said.

He took her in his arms to kiss her, gently at first, but it soon changed to an impassioned embrace. Their bodies twisted under the shower in an intimate wrestle. She yielded and molded to him.

She was breathless from the water beating down on them, astonished at how easily he became excited. There was no mistaking what was nudging her belly. She took hold of his penis and gave him a squeeze. He broke the kiss to look at her.

Holding his gaze, she began stroking him. She felt him getting bigger and applied a handful of soap to him, working up a creamy lather. She continued to pump him and loved seeing his expression as his arousal intensified.

Henrik squirted soap onto her breasts, kneaded them, and pinched her nipples. She purred with pleasure before he silenced her with his lips on hers. He transferred the soap to her pussy, vibrating her clit.

"Leah, I recall owing you a massage," he said.

She was reeling from his touch and barely able to stand up as he fondled her. After several minutes, he took the shower nozzle and sprayed the soapy foam off her body. She fell against the wall for support, and he moved with her.

Henrik knelt at the crux of her open legs. He cupped his mouth on her and extended his tongue to lick every fold. Leah groaned and welcomed the invasion. Henrik tapped her engorged bud, flicked it, and then fluttered atop it. She went crazy and couldn't breathe, feeling smothered by the misty heat.

He grabbed her ass with both hands, sucking her until she was about to explode. He inserted his finger in her anus, and she screamed. Her body convulsed in violent spasms, and he enveloped her thighs with his arms so she wouldn't slip and fall. Henrik drank from her until she stopped shaking.

Her legs eventually gave way, which caused her to slide down the tiled wall. Henrik sat in front of her, his back leaning against her. She wrapped her arms around his waist, allowing the water to rain on them. Peering over his shoulder through the steamy spray, she saw his cock, upright and swollen, ready for her.

They retreated to his bedroom and made furious love for the rest of the night, neglecting everything else they had planned. They probably got less than three hours sleep altogether. All she remembered was drifting off, only to be awakened by Henrik poking her with another hard-on, and soon they were at it again.

By morning, she was physically depleted and struggling to think straight. Though there was obvious affection between them, they were both quiet. Leah cleaned up the kitchen as Henrik packed his belongings. She helped him load the car, and he drove to her cabin. He got out to walk her to the door.

"Thank you, Leah, for the pleasure of meeting you ... and for so much more." He held her close.

She looked into his eyes, thinking it might be the last time she would ever see them. "I didn't do anything."

"Yes, you did. I had forgotten about my desires—you showed me how good it feels to want again."

She wanted to cry. "Henrik, I just wish you didn't have to leave. I—"

"It's okay. We don't need to have it all figured out right now."

"I know, but it would have been nice to have a few more days with you."

He kissed her, long and deep. "Leah, you came here to finish your book, right?"

"Yes."

"And you're well on your way now."

"With your help …"

"No, Leah, you did that on your own, and I know how important it is for you to complete it. We are …" He kissed her again. "We are good, I promise you."

"Are we?" She hated not having all the answers.

"Yes," he said. "I'll find my way back to you."

"But—"

"Leah … you're where my journey ends."

*   *   *   *

Hi, Mom,

Happy New Year! Sorry I didn't write sooner.

I want to thank you for your advice regarding Henrik. It really helped. He went home to Norway after Christmas Day. You could say we had a whirlwind romance. He literally swept me off my feet. I don't doubt my feelings for him anymore. As for our future together—I'm cautiously optimistic.

I've been writing up a storm and should be finished on schedule, if not sooner. After much thought, I've decided this will be my last book as H. J. Carlsen. It's time I laid him to rest—for good.

For the next chapter of my life, I thought I'd try romance novels. What do you think?

Love,

Leah

Leah sent off the e-mail to her mother and closed her laptop. Earlier in the day, she'd submitted the first six chapters of her book to her editor. She couldn't get over how much she had written. The best part was that she actually spent fewer hours writing each day yet accomplished more by the end of it. She owed a lot of her newfound energy to Henrik.

It was so clear to her now why she was able to write again after Henrik showed up. He'd turned her back on, and not just sexually. She had been living in a fog since Johan died. Her reality had become shrouded in her stories about larger-than-life characters who led extraordinary lives. Though she loved writing about adventure and all the excitement that went along with it, she had lost touch with her own needs. Her life in no way resembled the plots of her books, nor did she want it to.

Like Henrik, she had not been living life to its fullest, and her withdrawal from all the things she loved to do eventually depleted her creativity. She had stopped traveling and felt isolated from many of her friends and fellow writers. Those were the experiences that fed her stories. She realized that she didn't have to be a thrill seeker—she just had to live up to her potential. That, in itself, was the adventure.

Leah developed a new routine with the aim of rebalancing her life. She no longer opened her laptop upon waking up. Instead, she went for a two-hour hike. It gave her a chance to get outside and clear her mind so she could seize the day. Following that, she ate breakfast, reconnected with friends via e-mail, and began writing by nine. She was her most productive in the morning. After a break for lunch, she resumed writing until it got dark outside. Her newfound discipline forced her to turn the computer off by seven. This freed up her evenings to rediscover the things she had neglected—watching movies, reading, and preparing gourmet dinners for herself.

She was curled up on the couch in front of the fireplace, staring into the flames. It was difficult to believe the chain of events since she'd first arrived at Cedar Valley. She missed Henrik. Some nights her body yearned for him sexually, but there was something else she longed for: his sense of conviction.

Having spent most of the past eight years feeling unfit to be with anyone, Henrik told her he would rather go through life alone than be with the wrong person. It amazed her that he knew she was the right one for him the moment he kissed her. She realized her doubts were never about how she felt for him.

They had to do with her unreconciled feelings for Johan. Her initial thoughts were that Johan and Henrik had lived parallel lives, but in reality, it was *her* and Henrik who had walked similar paths.

Leah breathed in the scent of the fire and listened to the wind whistling outside. It was the same sound she had heard the morning Henrik left—more than a week ago already.

*   *   *   *

Leah arrived in Toronto amidst a blizzard. Far from the pristine white calm of Cedar Valley, she now had to contend with the gray, biting cold of the metropolitan city. The road crew had been dispatched well before rush hour, but the highway traffic was still horrendous. It took her a full hour to navigate the final leg of the drive into the downtown core—twice as long as normal. As she drew closer to her house, she could practically smell the chaos. It was the start of the workweek, and no one was happy to wake up to a snowstorm.

When she closed her front door after hauling in the last piece of luggage, she saw a vase of fresh daisies on the dining room table. Her mail was neatly stacked beside it, a handwritten note on top of the pile. It read:

> *Leah,*
> *Welcome back and congratulations on your book! I'm so proud of you and knew you could do it.*
> *I bought a few necessities for you and put them in the fridge. Call me when you get a moment.*
> *Love,*
> *Mom*

She felt so lucky to have her for her mother.

It took Leah a few hours to settle in. She did several loads of laundry, picked up her phone messages, and heated frozen lasagna for dinner. The drive had exhausted her, and she would need to get groceries before she was able to cook a decent meal.

By nightfall, the storm had passed, but there would be a lengthy cleanup process. In some areas of the city, they had lost power due to downed hydro lines. On her street, the winds had battered the old trees, leaving numerous small branches in the middle of the road. Leah felt at odds being in the city again. She was happy to be home, and she should have been over the moon with the success of her yet-to-be-released book, but all she could think about was Henrik and how much she missed him.

A lot of hype had been generated around the fact that *The Norwegian* was H. J. Carlsen's swan song. Because of that, most of Leah's back catalogue saw a resurgence in sales, which only increased her popularity and the anticipation for the upcoming book. Advance orders had already exceeded expectations. Her publisher had fast-tracked its printing and was confident it would be an immediate bestseller. It was launching in mid-March, and she was scheduled for a nationwide book tour—something she didn't normally like to do, but she looked forward to this one.

The Norwegian involved the rescue of a famous Canadian author who vacations at a ski resort in Geilo, Norway. A ransom note shows up at her publisher's office, demanding five million euros for her safe return. The police are initially tasked with delivering the money; however, the ransom exchange proves fatal. The drop-off is at a remote slope north of Oslo, where they are hit with an avalanche—killing both the police and the kidnappers. The body of the author is nowhere to be found.

The protagonist of the story is a former Olympian biathlete who is intimately familiar with the terrain. He has lived and trained there since childhood and knows the victim is being held somewhere in the mountains.

He is hired to lead a search party to find her. While laying the groundwork, he scrutinizes every aspect of the author's life and feels himself becoming strangely attracted to her. He realizes it is illogical to be falling for someone he has never met, which only makes him more determined to find her. He masterminds the plan for the rescue team, but they are unable to carry off the mission due to impending treacherous weather conditions. The hero eventually goes it alone, knowing that time is of the essence if he wants to find the author alive.

Leah didn't always write happy endings, but she did for this one. She felt it was the right thing to do as her final tribute to Johan. Both the dangerous mountain scenes and the man's fearless pursuit of a woman he barely knew were integral to the plot. The action sequences were easy to write—the love story difficult. In the past, Johan was her muse. This time, not only did someone else inspire her, but she was also painfully aware that this was the last book under H. J. Carlsen. She wanted to ensure the right balance of strength and vulnerability in her leading man. In the end, it seemed effortless stringing the right words together, but she was never more emotionally exhausted after completing a book.

Following dinner, Leah opened her laptop. She was anxious to find out her itinerary for the book tour. As usual, she was expected to go to the major Canadian and American cities, but she had requested a trip to Europe as well, particularly Norway. She reasoned that would be appropriate, as it was where the story took place. Secretly, she thought that would provide the opportunity to see Henrik again.

He had not been in touch. They hadn't exchanged e-mail addresses or phone numbers. She assumed his intention had been to respect her deadline, as he knew it was why she had gone to Cedar Valley in the first place. He'd assured her he would find her again, but when? She felt farther away from him now that she had finished her book, especially since she was no longer at the resort, where she was at least able to feel his presence.

Leah read the itinerary for her book tour. Canada: Toronto; Montreal; Vancouver. United States: New York; Chicago; Los Angeles. Europe: Paris; London; Oslo.

She was delighted to see Oslo on the list, but it was the last city on the tour. That meant she wouldn't be there until the end of March. How could she possibly wait so long?

*　　　*　　　*　　　*

Over the next couple of weeks, Leah's publicist scheduled interviews and photo shoots for the book tour. Leah had never enjoyed the business side of writing, but she understood how important it was to selling books.

There was already a lot of prelaunch press for *The Norwegian*. Early reviews for the book were positive. She had done a lengthy phone interview for the *New York Times Book Review*, and her book was among the reads for its Editors' Choice column.

The *Chicago Sun Times* wrote, "Will have you shivering with anticipation until the last page."

The *Globe and Mail*'s review: "Perhaps H. J. Carlsen's best book ... action will leave you chilled to the bone ... love story will heat you back up ..."

An endorsement for her book in the *Norway Post* made her chuckle: "H. J. Carlsen's depiction of the hero makes all Norwegian men proud."

Her good friend arranged to kick off the book tour. Pamela Dean helmed Pages, the largest bookstore in Toronto. Leah sat with Pam and drank tea as she waited to appear onstage. She had gone for a haircut earlier in the week and loved her new look. It was shorter than she had worn it in years, falling just above her shoulders. She wore high-heeled black boots with a burgundy wool dress that hugged her curves. A colorful string of crystal beads hung around her neck, and she had on minimal makeup.

"You look stunning," Pam said. "Are you nervous?"

"Thanks, and yes, I must admit I am a little. It's been sometime since I've done one of these. I guess I should feel lucky that I haven't had to promote my books in a while."

"I know, but it's good for business, good for both of us." Pam had worked her way up from being a store clerk to owning the second largest bookstore in Canada. Leah respected her judgment as an avid reader who was also a savvy businesswoman.

They agreed to do the *interview* setup—two chairs on the stage across from one another, with Pam playing talk show host to Leah's guest role. Leah much preferred this intimate format to simply standing on stage at a podium, reading excerpts from her book. She likened that method to delivering a lecture, something she was never comfortable with, even when she was teaching.

Leah never knew the mood or makeup of an audience prior to walking on stage, but they were typically fans, so she expected a friendly crowd. There was only one occasion when that was not the case, and it was when she killed off the lead character from her spy series. She had run out of ideas for him and didn't want to prolong the life of a stagnant character. Leah recalled a few hostile people in the audience that day, saying they would never buy her books again.

After Pam introduced her, she walked out to enthusiastic applause and perused the crowd. She recognized a few members of Pam's staff in the audience. They were there, as required, to warm up the audience by asking the first questions. Because her books were considered action-adventure thrillers, they had a wide appeal for both men and women. She was delighted to see that it was standing room only—about two hundred people packed into the small auditorium.

The interview portion was scheduled for thirty minutes. Leah had reviewed the list of questions beforehand. Most of them were geared toward people who were already fans of her novels, but there were some targeted to those who had not read any of her books. It was a way to provide them with some background about herself as a writer. Leah knew Pam's motivation was sales, and the more familiar people were with an author, the more likely they would buy her books.

"Ms. Carlsen, you have been writing under the same pseudonym for the past four years. It's a recognized brand. Why is this your last book as H. J. Carlsen?" Pam asked.

Leah took a deep breath before answering. She had told Pam to start with this question, as it was probably what her most devoted readers wanted to know.

"It was not an easy decision," she said. "H. J. Carlsen was the name of someone very important to me ... who died at an early age. Through my stories, he lived on, and I was able to mask my grief. I'm no longer grieving, so I felt it was the right time to let him go."

She could have heard a pin drop in the room.

"H. J. Carlsen was Norwegian, correct?"

"Yes."

"The hero of *The Norwegian* is one of the most vibrant characters you have ever written. Were you inspired by someone?"

"Yes, a special man."

"Care to elaborate?"

"Well ..." She laughed, noticing that Pam had ad-libbed on that question.

The audience urged her on.

"Let's just say I know he sounds too good to be true, but he isn't," Leah said. "You'll need to read the book to find out all his special qualities."

When the interview portion ended, the audience asked thoughtful questions about her motivation to write, how she came up with her stories, and whom she liked to read. The final question came from a young woman who asked what she intended to do next ... and whether she would continue to write.

"Funny you should ask that," Leah said. "I've been writing action thrillers for most of my career. Though I love this genre and do not intend to give it up entirely, I have been contemplating moving in a different direction. A while ago, I asked my mother if I should try my hand at romance novels. She thought it was a good idea."

The audience gave her a standing ovation. Leah could not have asked for a better way to begin her book tour.

She was slated to sign books for the next hour but was aware that it would take longer, as there was a huge line forming. Leah spent time acquainting herself with each reader who came up to her. She chatted with some, had her picture taken with others, and gave tips to young writers. Before she knew it, she had been signing books for almost two hours. The store was about to close. There were still a few people left.

Leah was tired but also energized from the whole experience. She had quite enjoyed it, and she was anxious to continue the tour. She would be flying to Montreal the day after next.

Pam came by as she was packing up. "There's one more customer who wants a signed copy. We've run out of books at the front. Do you have any with you?"

Leah got up to check the box behind her desk. "I can't believe you've run out," she said. "I have a few here."

"Okay, I'll tell him to come over."

Leah reached down to grab a copy and heard footsteps coming toward her. "Whom should I make it out to?" she asked.

"The man who found his way back to you."

She froze, fearful she had mistaken his voice. "Henrik?"

"Hello, Leah."

She slowly turned to see him standing there, looking more gorgeous than she remembered. His hair was longer, and he was dressed in a three-piece charcoal suit. His white shirt was unbuttoned at the top, and he was carrying a single red rose.

"This is for you," he said, holding out the flower for her. "Congratulations on the book."

She came out from behind the desk. "Thank you," she said, taking the soft petals to her nose to inhale the flower's sweet scent. "I'm so happy you're here. I missed you terribly."

Henrik moved close to her and brushed her cheek. "You weren't due in Oslo till the end of the month. I couldn't wait." He kissed her with the lips she had been dreaming of since she'd last seen him.

She wrapped her arms around his neck, pressing her body into his. When she opened her eyes, she realized the lights had dimmed.

Leah walked out of the store with the Norwegian.

the austrian and the asian

The first time Elena met Simon Bauer was in Phuket, Thailand, Christmas of 1988. She was visiting several countries in Asia after finishing university and prior to finding a job. She was two months into a trip she had budgeted to last for at least a year. Simon was with two friends—Julian Schmidt and Stefan Georges. They stayed at a small hotel not far from hers.

She was twenty-two and had never been outside of Canada. She met the three men on her second day at the popular beach resort while looking for somewhere to lay her towel. Simon offered to keep an eye on her bag so she could run in the ocean for a swim. When she returned for her things, she saw that he had found her a beach chair and set her up with them. For the rest of the week, they always made sure to secure a chair for her.

She had been trekking in Kathmandu prior to Thailand and was exhausted. A beach holiday was just what she needed. The Austrians were from a spa town called Baden, located approximately thirty-five kilometers outside of Vienna. Simon was the youngest at twenty-two, Julian was twenty-five, and Stefan was twenty-six. Friends from work, they were in Thailand on vacation. Simon was blond and outgoing and knew the least amount of English, yet somehow he had no problems communicating with her. With curly brown hair, Julian was like a teddy bear and laughed easily. He was the designated translator for the group since he had studied some English in school. Stefan was the serious one. Like his friends, he was over six feet tall. He had dark hair and made her feel uncomfortable with the way he glared at her. She couldn't tell if he didn't want her hanging out with them or whether it was just a language problem. After a couple of days, he became friendlier toward her. It was still awkward between them, but she assumed he was probably just a shy person.

Elena Lee was first-generation Chinese born in Canada. Though not as dark as the Thai girls, she was constantly being mistaken for one of them. She didn't mind, as it felt good to blend in, but she realized that once she opened her mouth, the locals immediately knew she was a foreigner. Fluent in English and French, she spoke a bit of German and Spanish as well. The way she dressed and her mannerisms also set her apart from the Thai.

She was petite with long, wavy black hair that reached the middle of her back, and she had almond-shaped eyes and full ruby lips. She was aware that the Austrians considered her extremely exotic when they confessed that she did not fit the mold of what they thought a Canadian looked like. She felt it was her duty to educate them on the demographics of her country. In doing so, she became their unofficial ambassador to Canada.

Ironically, she only came to understand the allure of being Asian during her travels. Coming from a multicultural city such as Toronto, she usually fit in—race was rarely an issue. She went to school with kids of every nationality, and being Asian was no different from being Greek, Italian, or German. She felt unique as a Chinese Canadian in Asia, and she had learned to appreciate the value of her Canadian passport.

Elena discovered many men were fascinated by Asian women and went to places such as Thailand, Indonesia, or the Philippines to find suitable wives. She quickly learned the clichés, having admittedly been incredibly naive prior to her trip. She abhorred the China doll stereotype, portraying Asian women as subservient, domestic, and eager to please in bed. She felt it was a matter of circumstance, wherein third world women—because of societal forces and not individual choice—were sometimes compelled to sell themselves to support their families.

Coming from the West, she was not subservient nor more domesticated than any of her non-Asian girlfriends. As for her willingness in bed, her limited experience had taught her she could be good with the right man—it had nothing to do with being Asian. The stereotypes only dehumanized women living in the East, yet she was amazed at how many men held those same beliefs about her, even though she was Canadian.

Thankfully, the Austrians did not have those misconceptions. They thought she was extremely brave to travel on her own. Elena knew they admired her independence but still felt protective of her. She didn't take offence to that and quite liked their gallantry.

In the evenings, she accompanied them barhopping along the Phuket strip. She wasn't a big drinker but enjoyed the atmosphere of the international crowd. The Austrians followed her lead in how best to charm the Thai people. Because she was never demanding, unlike other tourists, they received the best service wherever they went.

Toward the last days of their stay, Elena noticed that both Simon and Stefan had taken a liking to her. There seemed to be a healthy competition for her affection between them. She observed little things like fighting for who got her a drink on the beach or who sat next to her for meals. Julian, who had a girlfriend back in Austria, told her how amused he was to watch his two friends battle for her.

The two men had such distinctly different approaches. Simon was showy and confident. Because he couldn't really speak with her, he was physical with his affection. He touched her often, and he made her laugh with his silly antics of falling in the sand as if he had been struck with Cupid's arrow. He took her out Jet Skiing and pulled her in the ocean for swims.

Stefan was the complete opposite—he was quiet. When he did talk to her in English, he spoke steadily and with great effort, trying hard to pronounce the words properly. She suspected he had Julian script what he wanted to say. He was not as open with his affection as Simon, but she found his awkward attempts to communicate with her even more appealing.

One night, Stefan bought her a string of orchids when they were all out at a club. He told her the pink and white strand of flowers reminded him of her—small and sensitive. She didn't know what he meant at first, but in talking to Julian, she realized he wanted to say that she was small and *delicate*. She thought it was sweet of him to see her that way, even though she never considered herself delicate. She wore the flowers around her neck. Not to be outdone, Simon bought her two strings of orchids. Of course, she had to wear them too. If there was any hint of jealousy, Stefan didn't show it. She enjoyed the attention while it lasted.

It was a wonderful week with the Austrians, and when it came time to say good-bye, they exchanged addresses and phone numbers. Elena promised to write.

*   *   *   *

After meeting so many people from Europe who invited her to stay with them, Elena decided to extend her journey and do a tour there before flying home to Canada. She anticipated that it could be years before she had such an opportunity to travel again. Following the end of her Asian trip, she planned to visit five European countries where she had formed strong friendships. It was early December of 1990 when she arrived in Austria. It was also her final destination. She had planned to stay just the month, with the intention of ringing in the New Year back in Toronto. She had been corresponding periodically with her mother since her departure. From what Elena could gather, nothing much had changed, not when compared to what she had experienced. Nevertheless, she felt somewhat homesick and longed to see her family and friends again.

When she arrived in Austria, Julian and Stefan were there to greet her at the airport. She would be staying with Stefan in his house, using it as her base to see other parts of Austria. She had contacted Simon as well but never heard from him. Julian told her he had changed jobs, and they had lost touch with him as well.

It was cold winter weather, and there was snow on the ground, but fortunately, she was still able to get away with wearing sneakers. That was a good thing since she didn't have a pair of boots with her. She also didn't have a winter coat, so Stefan lent her one of his—a leather jacket that resembled a trench coat on her.

Stefan stood a foot taller than Elena, with wide shoulders, a massive chest, and long, muscular legs. His jet-black hair was not as wavy as she remembered, but his dark eyes were as intense as when they'd first met. In the tropics, she had already been attracted to him, recalling how his piercing stare had unsettled her. He still looked at her the same way, but she was used to it now. He smiled readily with her, which softened his gaze. The fact that he had offered up his house proved to her that he was at least comfortable in her presence.

Stefan's hospitality was unlike any she had experienced on her travels. He gave her a key, and she was free to come and go as she pleased. His house was a two-bedroom townhome, quite big by Canadian standards. She liked the layout and the way he had decorated it in muted tones of brown and gray. It was masculine without being overtly stark. An architect, he had a keen sense of design.

After sleeping in the guest bedroom the first night she arrived, Elena left the next morning to go skiing in the western regions of Austria. She rented a car and drove to Salzburg and Innsbruck. Stefan had already left for work before she awoke, so she did not see him.

After a week and a half, she returned to Baden to spend Christmas with Stefan. Her room was neat and tidy, just as she had left it, save for a fresh vase of pink and white orchids by the bed. She thought it was sweet and wondered if it was a coincidence that Stefan chose those particular flowers. Had he remembered buying them for her in Phuket? She never asked him, but she suspected he wasn't one for coincidences.

On her first night back, she and Stefan met up with Julian and his girlfriend, Martina, for dinner at a *Heurigen*—an Austrian wine tavern. It was fantastic to reconnect with Julian. Either her German had improved or their English had gotten better, for they had no problems understanding one another. They did so with a combination of the two languages, butchering both grammatically, but it didn't matter. After a few glasses of wine, they all seemed to be speaking the same language anyway.

She was feeling tipsy by the time Stefan drove her back to his place. He, however, was the consummate gentleman, as she remembered from Thailand. After making her a cup of tea, they discussed what she would like to see while in his country. It was the weekend, and he had taken a week off work to be her personal tour guide. Elena was really touched by that. When she turned in for the night, he came to her door and assured her that she was safe with him.

She lay awake thinking whether the communication lines were crossed. She yearned for something more than just safety.

*   *   *   *

Elena had been staying with Stefan for almost a week now. The chemistry between them was electric, but he had not made any advances toward her. She wasn't sure if he felt it inappropriate to make a move because she was his guest.

Did his staunch, Austrian conservatism prevent him from taking advantage of her? Was there perhaps some cultural divide she was unaware of?

She was just coming into her own sexual awareness. Her traditional Asian upbringing had always taught her to be polite, gracious, and humble. She didn't want to appear too aggressive, but try as she might, she couldn't contain her lustful thoughts. Every night, she fell asleep thinking of ways to seduce him.

They had just come back to Stefan's house after Christmas Eve dinner. She'd met his parents and Stefan's brother and his family. Initially, she felt nervous about meeting them as she didn't want to impose on a family holiday, but Stefan was so attentive to her that she was soon at ease.

They had a lovely meal in the Austrian tradition. Fried carp was the main course, and she was surprised at how much she liked it. Stefan's father introduced her to *Glühwein*, a mulled wine, and she gorged herself on homemade Sachertorte—a rich chocolate apricot cake. She ate three pieces along with other chocolate delicacies, including edible Christmas ornaments. Her healthy appetite amazed his family, and she ended up having a great time with them.

Elena was changing when she heard footsteps approach her bedroom. Every evening, Stefan would come to her bedroom to say good night. They had developed a funny little game in the form of a knock-knock joke. She had taught him the pattern of the joke, but he couldn't understand the humor. Even though she had grown up with the jokes as a kid, she never found them particularly funny. For some reason though, they took on a comical turn when she told them to Stefan. Tonight, he was there again.

"Knock, knock," he said, as he tapped on her door.

"Who's there?" she asked.

"Stefan."

"Stefan who?"

"Stefan here to say good night."

She wore her slinkiest satin nightgown, which exposed just enough of her modest cleavage. She quickly looked in the mirror, tousled her hair, and pinched her cheeks.

Elena opened the door and didn't hide behind it as she had in previous nights. She gave him full view of her lithe body and could see he was taken with her.

"So … it's not Stefan, the big bad wolf?" she asked with a flirtatious lilt.

"No," he said, promptly reverting to his stoic expression.

"Oh, that's too bad." Elena saw he was blushing. She felt slightly embarrassed for flaunting herself, but she didn't regret getting a rise out of him.

"I wish you a good sleep and sweet dreams."

"Thank you, Stefan, and sweet dreams to you too." She stood on her toes to peck him on the cheek. "*Gute Nacht*," she said.

"Good night, Elena."

She closed the door slowly and didn't take her hand off the knob for some time. She was disappointed. He was a gentleman, and that's what she liked about him, but he was driving her crazy. She still felt him standing on the other side of the door. She was certain she'd heard his heart thumping out of his chest when she kissed him. It seemed like minutes before he walked away toward his bedroom. It required all her strength not to run after him. She was wet just envisioning him in the room down the hall. If only he would knock again, she wouldn't hesitate to invite him into bed with her.

Elena crawled beneath the blankets, unable to stop thinking of him. She had never been so turned on by any man. Stefan was little more than a stranger, someone she had known for only two weeks. Where she was free and easygoing, he was courteous, bordering on standoffish. They were worlds apart culturally, yet she was so attracted to him.

She wrote in her journal and read a few chapters of her book before turning out the light. Thoughts of Stefan fogged the landscape of her mind, and she was unable to fall asleep. Outside, she heard the cold Austrian wind rattling the tree branches. Inside, she felt hot and kicked off the blanket, sleeping only in her thin nightgown.

There was a knocking sound. Had she really heard it, or was it only wishful thinking? She wasn't sure, but then she heard the doorknob turning. She saw a person enter the room and move in her direction. She tried calling out to ask who it was, but no sound escaped from her.

She sensed the weight of someone on the bed. She imagined it to be Stefan and it excited her—she wanted him.

Hands pushed up her nightgown, exposing her thighs, her mound, and her breasts. She tried to raise her head, but it was impossible—it felt like lead.

Fingers fondled her snatch and gently grazed her labia. She arched her back when lips touched her slit. Elena was powerless to hide her need.

Although able to squirm, her limbs remained immobilized. Without warning, a force lifted her buttocks to become more intimate with her lover. His mouth encircled her swollen pussy, and a prodding tongue licked up and down her vulva. She felt dizzy and welcomed the violation after nights of pent-up lust. He sucked her tender folds and nuzzled around her clit, unhurried at first, but then he ate her with the hunger of a starving man. Her breasts were on fire and every nerve in her body cried out for release.

As if her thoughts were wishes to be obeyed, Elena's invisible shackles magically disappeared, and she was able to grope and tweak her nipples until they stood pointy and erect. She writhed under the pleasure of the sensual massage at her loins.

He gulped her secretions and encircled her engorged nub to flick it—she rocked in an animated tremble, feeling faint and ready to explode. One final tap and she saw stars as the swells of her orgasm gushed through her being.

Elena woke up to hear a cry of unabashed passion. Her scream cut through the stillness of the night, and it took several minutes to regain her composure. She covered up with the blanket and touched the stickiness between her legs—a wet dream—she couldn't recall the last time she'd had one. She had drenched the sheets. Staying with Stefan was sending her libido into overdrive. She decided what she had to do.

*   *   *   *

At dawn, Elena wrapped her naked body in a blanket and tiptoed to Stefan's room. She enclosed her palm around the doorknob, and for a brief moment, she was afraid the door was locked. She turned slowly, held her breath, and pushed. It was the first time she saw the inside of his bedroom.

It was dark and quiet. She crouched by Stefan's bed and sat against the wall. He was facing her in a fetal position, and he looked peaceful. She let her vision adjust to the darkness of the room and saw that it was very spare. Aside from the bed, there were two night tables and a pants press in the corner.

She drew up her knees and rested her chin on them, hugging her legs to keep warm. She ogled Stefan as he slept. There was no plan whatsoever should he wake up. The only thing she was certain about was how inflamed she felt.

Elena shifted on the floor and began counting Stefan's breaths as he inhaled. He fascinated her, and she wanted to be near him if only just to feel him breathing. When he exhaled on his eighteenth breath, he opened his eyes. He looked stunned. She didn't dare move as she watched him come to the realization of her sitting by his bedside. Time stood still. In his sleepy, shocked state, he reached for her without saying a word.

She dropped her blanket on the floor and allowed him to pull her into bed with him. She loved how he engulfed her with his warmth under the sheets. Her cool hands caressed his chest, and she felt him shiver. Soon his heat radiated to her, intensifying her desire for him—she was burning up.

She urged him onto his back and draped herself over him. She was probably half his weight, and he supported her easily. He wore a pair of boxers, but they could not hide the fact he was already hard.

"Close your eyes," she said to him in German.

She brushed her lips atop his long eyelashes before moving to his eyelids, across his forehead, and to his ears. He enclosed her in his arms as she slid to his neck, traveling downward. She placed her palm on his chest and felt the strength of his heartbeat. She kissed his nipples, sucking each one until they hardened. He growled when she scraped her nails along the sides of his waist.

Elena curled her fingers under the waistband of his boxers. She looked up to see him staring at her before she pulled his shorts off and tossed them on the floor. She was mesmerized by his erection, having never been with anyone so big before.

She wanted to tell him how beautiful he was but didn't know the exact German words to convey it, so she said part of it in English and hoped he would understand. "Stefan, your penis is so big. *Es ist phantastisch.*"

His cock stood up straight and was already glistening with excitement. He was at least seven inches and extremely thick. The sight of him made her tingle all over, and she knew she wanted to seduce him. She had dreamt about it all night. She grasped him firmly and bent to taste the salty liquid oozing out of him. He propped himself up on his forearms and swept her hair away from her face. She could tell he wanted to watch her.

She gave him feathery kisses all over before licking him under the ridge.

Back and forth, she moved her lips across his shaft, creating a slippery, wet surface before she gently pumped him, delighting in how he grew harder. Stefan let go of her hair and sank deep into his pillow.

She proceeded to stroke him and reached to touch his upper body, rubbing his broad chest. He had just the right amount of hair for her liking—it was fuzzy and soft. She grabbed a fistful and tugged on it to feel Stefan flinch before releasing her hold. She pinched his nipples and lightly tickled his taut abdomen until she saw him shudder.

Stefan's cock was throbbing in her hand, yet she wanted to tease him just a bit longer. Probing further, she surrounded his testicles to massage them against the roof of her mouth. It was something she had never done, but she was captivated by his arousal and felt compelled to explore every inch of him.

Elena could not wait to feast upon him. Holding tight, she enclosed her lips over him and slowly took him in. Moving in a circular motion, she glided downward to the base until he hit the back of her gullet before she slid up again. Moments later, she was bobbing her head and swirling her tongue on top of his engorged rim. He grew even bigger.

"*Mein Gott* ...," he said.

Elena relaxed her muscles with Stefan lodged in the abyss of her throat. She purred continuously to create vibrations around his knob. Soon she sensed tremors coming from his balls. He clutched the bedsheets before she felt him tense up. He let out an impassioned groan as he started to shake, flooding her with his hot cum. She gulped him up, unable to get enough of how sweet he tasted.

It took awhile before Stefan stopped coming ... and even longer before he went limp. She leisurely ascended him, nibbling all the way up. Lying on top of him, Elena rested her ear on his chest to listen to the fast-paced beating of his heart.

Stefan kissed the top of her head. "I thank you so very much for that," he said, sighing and trying to regain his breath.

She let out a giggle and rested her chin on his chest to look at him. "You are very welcome. It was my pleasure." She never recalled any previous boyfriends thanking her for a blow job. "You had so much inside, and I needed time to drink you up."

He seemed embarrassed. "It was too much?"

"*Nein*, Stefan, you can never be too much for me."

There was a softness in his eyes as he gazed at her. "Elena, I am never with Asian girl before. You are beautiful."

She found his broken English endearing. "Stefan, I have never been with an Austrian man, and you are beautiful too."

*   *   *   *

That evening, she made a meal of orange-almond salad, stir-fried chicken, and rice. Stefan loved the Asian flair she put into her cooking. It was quite ironic considering she didn't prepare much of it when she was at home. Afterward, he insisted on cleaning up since she'd made dinner. She was nervous, as she wanted so much to be with him, but she didn't want to appear presumptuous. He had not made any mention of a change in sleeping arrangements. As he put the dishes away, she went into her room to read.

An hour later, she was tired and decided to get ready for bed. She stepped out to go to the bathroom. There was no sign of Stefan. She noticed there was light flickering from underneath the door of his bedroom, and it was quiet. She returned to her room feeling rejected and discouraged. Had she assumed too much?

They had spent a lovely day together in Vienna, sightseeing and shopping, and she knew the chemistry between them had only grown stronger. Now, it seemed, she was back to square one. Elena lay naked in bed, confused and wondering whether she had insulted Stefan in some way.

Her confusion soon changed to depression and then to anger. For some reason, she almost felt used even though *she* was the one who had made the first move, and he had been more than willing to accommodate her. She had no reason to be angry, except that she wanted more, and she couldn't understand why he was ignoring her. As she continued to think about it, she became increasingly furious. Just as she was about to storm out of her room and give Stefan a piece of her mind, she heard a tap on the door.

"Elena?"

She immediately felt her heart race. "Yes ... one moment, please." She jumped out of bed and didn't even bother putting on her nightgown, choosing instead to swathe herself in a bedsheet. When she opened the door, she saw

Stefan standing there with a small paper bag. Wearing a white waffle cotton robe, he looked sexy as hell.

"Hi, Stefan," she said.

"I hope you are not yet sleeping?"

"No, just reading."

"Good. I buy a present for you today." He handed her the package.

She was moved by his gesture and ashamed for feeling so upset just moments earlier. "What is this?"

"Please open it."

She pulled something red and smooth from the bag. It was a silk robe in the style of a kimono.

"Stefan … this is beautiful." She had told him red was her favorite color. She rubbed the delicate cloth against her cheek. "Thank you."

"I think it is nice for you in the house, and—"

"And?"

"And I hope you also wear it to my bedroom."

Elena had to admit that was the most erotic invitation she'd ever received. She let the bedsheet drop to the floor, standing naked before him while he devoured her with his eyes. She gave him the kimono and allowed him to put it on for her. When she turned back to face him, he tied the sash.

She slid her palms under his robe, unable to control her lust—his skin was on fire. He swept her up into his arms, and she nestled her head against his shoulder. She trembled with desire as he carried her the short distance to his bedroom.

Elena saw fresh sheets on the bed and the room lit by at least a dozen candles placed around the windowsills.

"Stefan, the room is so beautiful."

By the time he laid her down on the bed, she was already desperate for him. In contrast to her impatience, Stefan was unhurried and methodical.

"You are so small, and I am so big," he said after he untied the kimono and exposed her.

It struck her as funny that he was so fascinated by their difference in size, but she let him discover her at his own pace. He was deliberately slow as he touched her flawless porcelain skin and long soft hair. He equally enamored her. His hairy chest and limbs aroused her, and she couldn't get enough of his firm body. She had never experienced such a patient lover.

He smothered her with his kisses, but she ached for so much more. She felt his hardness between her legs and wanted him inside her that instant. As if he were able to read her mind, he created a trail down her bosom with his tongue.

He kneaded her breasts, and gripped her nipples to caress them with his thumbs. He lingered there and teased her. She breathed heavily and grabbed onto the wrought iron panel behind her, arching herself toward the ceiling. Stefan was driving her crazy, but she loved the sweet agony of his foreplay. Elena was in heaven when he finally sucked her sensitive peaks into his mouth, tickling and licking them in the most painfully slow manner.

Stefan zigzagged his way across her, nipping her navel before he spread her legs farther apart with his knees. She had been wet for some time and couldn't wait for him to touch her pussy.

He rested her calves on top of his shoulders and bent forward to look at her neatly trimmed and protruding mound. It was slick with anticipation. Elena raised her head to watch as Stefan probed apart her labia and stroked all along her slit. She could feel his hunger for her.

She closed her eyes and relinquished control. Without warning, he penetrated her with two fingers, and she cried out with desire. He fondled her and she contracted around him—she'd never imagined she could feel so good.

"Stefan ... please—*bitte* ... eat me ..."

Stefan plummeted into her. He was ruthless, jabbing her hole continuously. He grasped her buttocks and pulled her closer to consume more of her. Elena knew she had unleashed the animal in him.

When her whimpers escalated, he enveloped her clit. She sensed a burning heat in her midsection, unlike anything she had ever experienced. Stefan poked and fluttered against her bud, alternating between gentleness and brutality—she lost it.

Elena convulsed and splashed Stefan's face, overpowered by wave after wave of bliss. Stefan cupped her with his mouth. Just when she thought she had finished coming, he reinserted his tongue. It was sublime.

From deep within, she felt the rumble of another eruption. She rocked the bed with the intensity of her climax, and it immediately made her weak. Stefan buried himself in her depths until she stopped trembling. When he made his way back up to her, she saw he was covered in her cum. She sucked his lips, reveling in the taste of her own juices.

"My god, Stefan ... *du bist wunderbar.*"

She was dazed from the turbulence of her orgasms. It was then that Stefan's knob bumped her stomach. She saw his need for her.

He opened the night table drawer and took out a condom, watching her all the while.

"Let me help you," she said. She'd never wanted anyone so much.

"I want you on top of me, Elena." He sat up against the headboard and placed a pillow behind him, extending his legs across the bed. He held his shaft at the base and watched as she positioned herself facing him.

Elena put her hands on his shoulders and hovered her pussy over his massive hard-on. At first, she allowed only the tip of him to enter, almost afraid he was too big. She closed her eyes, luxuriating in the initial feel of his insertion. Cautiously, she sat down on him. When he was firmly planted inside her, she let out a sigh and remained still for several moments. His penetration was absolute. Stefan leaned in to kiss behind her ears and her neck.

She began a slow swivel with her hips. Her muscles pulsated around him, and Stefan's desire expanded further. She started sliding on his pole, rising up just to the tip of him before plunging back down. At times, she even felt his balls slapping against her.

Elena locked eyes with Stefan as she rode him. The intensity of his stare excited her. She refused to blink, as she didn't want to miss a moment of his expression. She loved how his large hands cradled her ass. When he squeezed her buttocks, she bucked more forcefully. Her movements grew erratic, and she sensed a finger at her anus. When he slipped it in, she was swept away again. In that instant, Stefan picked her up with his cock still lodged inside and flipped her over. Holding one leg beside his shoulder, he drilled her with a savage-like fierceness. She felt his fiery poker buried high in her stomach.

Elena gasped for air and begged for relief from the tremors coursing through her. She turned her head and bit down on the pillow to stifle her scream.

He speared her so deeply that she almost passed out. When he came, his body jerked violently. She saw him close his eyes in torturous pleasure, grunting words that were neither comprehensible in English nor German.

She could never have guessed how passionate he was. They made love every night. Despite their many differences, she connected with him in a way she didn't think was possible, bridging language, racial, and cultural differences.

*   *   *   *

Elena extended her trip and brought in the New Year in Austria. It was approaching mid-January and getting colder. Her days were spent on long walks in Baden or in Vienna sightseeing while Stefan was at work. When he got home, they were inseparable. Sometimes she cooked for him, or he took her out to his favorite places for dinner. When they did go out, they often got curious glances from people because Stefan towered over her. One evening, they bumped into an old friend of his who thought she was a Thai girl he had sponsored for marriage. She found it quite humorous but knew that her looks were exotic to most Austrians. Elena realized it didn't matter to Stefan, as he was always affectionate with her in public.

She improved her German, and he improved his English. Their conversations were no longer just niceties about the weather or what she did during the course of the day. She conversed with him in German about current events and other world issues. She knew they had reached a completely new level of communication when they were able to share jokes.

"Knock, knock," he said to her one night, out of the blue, as they were having dinner.

His entry into the joke was so abrupt she almost choked on her food. She played along. "Who's there?"

"The Gestapo."

She grinned and took a gulp of water. "The Gestapo who?"

"We are the Gestapo. We never knock!"

She spit her drink all across the table, shocking Stefan with her unladylike outburst. She was immediately embarrassed by what she did.

"I am happy I make you laugh so much with my joke," he said.

"That was a great one, Stefan." She wiped away tears. "I'm sorry I made a mess."

"No problem. I finish already eating."

She kissed him, amused by how pleased he looked with himself. She experienced the nuances of how language and delivery of a joke could make it so much funnier. Even though he was far from mastering either, she loved him for trying and laughed easily with him.

They talked about many things, but the one topic they both avoided was what would happen once she went back to Canada. It had crossed her mind to stay longer, but she had already extended her trip once, and she wasn't doing it again—her humility wouldn't allow it. She was not only a guest in Stefan's country but also a guest in his house. She couldn't speculate if he wanted more than what they had while she was with him. Elena figured Stefan would ask her to postpone her departure if he really wanted her to stay.

On the day before she was scheduled to fly out, there was a huge snowstorm, and she secretly hoped that might thwart her plans to leave. Stefan didn't go into the office either, instead working on his drawings from home. She felt extremely melancholy, but she didn't let him know.

She went through his CD collection for something to console herself. He had plenty of classical music, which she normally enjoyed listening to, but she was not in the mood for it. He only had two compact discs that contained English music. One was the Beatles—the second was a collection of different artists. The popular singer she recognized on that album was Rod Stewart. The song on the disc was "I Don't Want to Talk About It."

When she put it on, she immediately choked up. In listening to the lyrics, she heard the words she was unable to voice to Stefan. The song expressed what her heart was feeling. She didn't want to leave him, but if she were to stay just another day, a week, or even a month, would that make a difference? Would he realize how much she loved him after that?

On the day of Elena's departure, the skies were clear, and it was sunny. Unfortunately for her, the storm had passed. The only promise she and Stefan made to each other was to write. As her plane took off and Austria disappeared below her, she started to cry.

*   *   *   *

After being away for almost two years, Elena was anxious to re-establish her life. Within a couple of months of returning to Canada, she found a job, and not long after that, she met someone new.

Mike was a photographer, sixteen years her senior, and traveled many of the same countries she had just visited. They began as friends, but it soon became obvious he wanted something more. She wasn't ready to commit, not while her heart still ached for Stefan.

They continued to exchange infrequent letters about how their lives were going, but they wrote little about their feelings for one another. Elena waited for Stefan to declare his love for her, to beg her to come back, or to confess he'd made a mistake by allowing her to leave.

Around that time, Mike was pressuring her to make a decision. He didn't know all the details concerning her Austrian boyfriend—only that she was torn between the two of them. Mike called her daily to convince her he was a better choice given all the obstacles of a long-distance relationship. He had the advantage of being able to react to her immediately, either in person or by phone. For months, Elena wrestled with her emotions. She was exhausted from sitting on the fence. In the end, the availability of someone to fill the void left by Stefan took precedence over waiting for his letters.

She elected to play it safe and stayed in the city to make a go of it with Mike. A month after Christmas, she moved in with him. She did not send a change of address to Stefan and stopped writing to him altogether. Even though she had her mail redirected from her apartment, she never received another letter from him. She assumed he had lost interest once she ended their correspondence.

She and Mike would eventually be together for close to a decade. It was good for a while, but she found out late in their relationship that he had been cheating on her. His neediness and deceitful nature were the reasons she finally put an end to it.

When the separation was complete, she fell into a deep depression that lasted months. Their union had robbed her of her self-worth, cheerful disposition, and desire to ever be in another long-term commitment.

*   *   *   *

Elena was back in Austria for the first time in over ten years. While planning her trip, she thought about reconnecting with Stefan but didn't feel right about it. He was probably married with kids, and she didn't want to disturb his life. She'd never forgotten him, though, and it pained her to think about the choice she'd made and what she'd done—especially now.

She took off two weeks over the Christmas holidays to undergo a kind of emotional convalescence. It was the year she turned thirty-five—a milestone marking some major changes in her life. She had recently ended her toxic relationship with Mike, quit her job, and sold her house, moving into a downtown two-bedroom condominium. She didn't want to stay in Toronto during the holidays, even though she'd had numerous offers for Christmas dinners and parties. The stress of the season only made things worse for her. In better times, she would have spent the holidays with Mike's family, but that wasn't an option anymore. In the end, she was convinced the best thing was to take a vacation on her own.

Elena held only the fondest memories of Austria, and she'd always known she would one day return. The fact that Stefan might still live there was certainly a draw for her, but the chances of running into him were remote. She merely wanted to recapture some of the good memories and feelings she'd experienced when she was there previously, and she realized she owed much of that to Stefan.

As she was not an expert skier, Elena found the Austrian Alps perfect for her. She chose a resort in the spa town of Bad Gastein. It had spectacular panoramas and a variety of pistes. It also boasted a waterfall above jagged cliffs and seventeen natural springs with healing waters—both indoor and outdoor. Its Belle Époque buildings were perched on towering precipices, and some of the larger hotels were built on various levels and connected by stairs, elevators, and small alleyways. The mix of international ski resort and health spa was exactly what she was looking for.

From the moment Elena arrived, she sensed the magical charm of Bad Gastein. The abundance of snow in the village and on the slopes created a glistening winter wonderland. Well laid out with mountain huts and restaurants, it was the best skiing she had ever done. She also took full advantage of the thermal baths at every opportunity.

The festive season was evident all around her. There was a huge decorated Christmas tree in the middle of the Gastein valley, along with white lights strung up in the nearby shops. Every night, there were fireworks and a street party in the middle of town. She couldn't think of anywhere else in the world she would rather be.

She also lucked out with her accommodations. She'd found a private company for vacation rentals and connected directly with the owner. Though advertised as an apartment, Elena thought of it more as a chalet. Set in a quiet part of town less than a ten-minute walk from the center, it was big enough for four people. It had a balcony overlooking the Alps and a traditional log-style fireplace with convenient access to skiing and the springs. The owner agreed to rent it for slightly less than the usual price because he preferred her to a rowdy group of students. Elena had not quite gotten used to downsizing from a large house to a condo and wanted to treat herself on this trip.

A couple of days before Christmas, she decided to take a break from skiing and do some sightseeing. She snapped some pictures of the waterfall and was delighted to hear a string and wind quartet playing nearby. She purchased a cup of Glühwein and sat on a bench to observe the festivities. The wine was hot and flavorful; its aroma sparked cherished memories of the Christmas she'd spent with Stefan's family.

She enjoyed the performance and took some pictures of the musicians. Soon people danced in the streets, and she photographed them as well. When someone motioned for her to join the group, she decided she had no reason to decline. The anonymity of being in a foreign country made her forget the pain of the past year, and she was not afraid to let her hair down. She finished her drink and joined the crowd in a dancing circle, feeling giddy and hypnotized by the pristine surroundings.

"Elena!"

She heard her name echo through the crowd and turned to see who'd yelled it, not expecting she was the actual subject of the call. She couldn't identify anyone.

"Elena, over here!"

She scanned the crowd again and saw a man waving at her. She glanced behind her to see if he was calling to someone else. Before she knew it, he was walking in her direction. It was only when he was within ten feet of her that she realized who it was.

"Julian!" She was stunned to see him.

"Wow, Elena, I cannot believe it's you!" He gave her a huge bear hug, lifting her off her feet.

"Julian, I can't believe it either."

"What are you doing here? Are you on holiday? Are you with friends?"

Julian's questions were fired at her like bullets from a gun. She felt almost obligated to tell him everything right on the spot. Just then, a small boy of about six came running up beside them. Julian picked him up in his arms.

"Felix, this is my friend, Elena. Say hello, please," he said in German.

"*Hallo*," Felix said enthusiastically.

"My goodness, he looks just like you!" She shook Felix's extended hand and remarked on how precocious he was. "Julian, he is absolutely adorable."

"Thank you. Martina is here too."

"Nice! How is she doing? Where is she?" Elena searched for her in the direction Julian had come from.

"She is well, but she stayed at the hotel with our daughter today."

"A daughter too?" Her heart melted a bit at how much time had passed. "That's so lovely. What's her name?"

"Sarah."

"What a beautiful name. I'm so happy for you, Julian."

"Thanks. Elena, you are here alone?"

"Yes."

"You always travel by yourself," he said with a chuckle. "You must have dinner with us tonight."

"No, no, you are here with your family."

"That doesn't matter. Martina would love to see you. Please join us. I want to hear about your life."

Elena winced at the thought of revealing all that had happened since she was last in Austria. She wasn't sure if Julian still kept in touch with Stefan.

"Julian—"

"Please, Elena. We go home to Baden tomorrow. It will be our only chance to get together before we leave."

He was so gracious and genuine, reminding her of the wonderful hospitality of the Austrian people.

"Okay …," she conceded. "I would like that very much."

She took down the name of their hotel as Julian hoisted Felix up onto his shoulders and walked off toward the slopes. She had come all this way to be by herself. Though she was thrilled to see Julian again, she knew her past was catching up with her. Until that moment, she'd never really grasped how small the world was.

*   *   *   *

With her curly blond locks, Sarah was precious and the spitting image of Martina. She and Felix were being put to bed when Elena arrived at their hotel. Martina's teenage niece had also come for the trip to help with the kids, and tonight she was staying with them so the adults could go out for dinner. They walked to a nearby restaurant.

"You look the same, like ten years before," Martina said to Elena. "Asian people do not get old!"

Elena smiled and blushed. She remembered that Martina's English was not very good, but they had never had a problem understanding one another.

For the next couple of hours, over a meal of Wiener schnitzel, spaetzle, and two bottles of red wine, they reminisced. She was guarded about her personal life where it concerned Stefan, but she let them know she had recently broke up with her boyfriend, had never married nor had kids. She'd left banking and was pursuing a career in writing.

She caught up with their lives, which revolved mainly around their children. Julian had climbed the corporate ladder and was now senior director of a software development company, while Martina was a stay-at-home mom. They'd only recently started to travel again since it was difficult with two young children to go far. They had been at the resort for the last week and planned to have a big Christmas celebration in Baden with Julian's family.

It was almost like old times, yet something was missing. When she was previously in Austria, she and Stefan socialized on numerous occasions with Julian and Martina. They were two happy couples back then. She definitely felt Stefan's absence now.

"Would you like to see pictures of our house?" Martina asked.

"Of course. Is it new?"

"Yes, we have builders make it for us, and it finished only in November."

Martina retrieved photographs from her purse and gave them to Elena. The house was magnificent. It was surrounded by forest and had a swimming pool and gardens. The interior was massive and airy, with plenty of light streaming in from the skylights.

"Martina, this is incredible. I love the design."

"Yes, you know Stefan make the plans for us."

Elena immediately sensed a tremor up her spine. It was the first mention of Stefan all evening. She kept her cool, trying not to sound overly anxious in an effort to find out more about him.

"Yes ... Stefan was an architect, of course," she said.

"He is one of the best in Austria. We were lucky to have him draw our house," Martina replied.

Elena was truly happy for how their lives had turned out, and a part of her lamented that she was now on her own. She wondered if Stefan ever told them what had happened between them, and *what* he would have told them.

She and Julian ordered Viennese coffee and *Apfelstrudel*, but Martina decided to call it a night.

"I think I drink too much wine," she said with a laugh.

Elena stood up at the table with her and hugged their good-byes. "I am so happy to see you again, Martina. If you come to Canada, it would be my pleasure to have you stay with me."

"Okay, you give e-mail address to Julian and we keep in contact."

"Yes, I promise to stay in touch this time." And she meant it.

Julian accompanied Martina to the hotel and returned just as the waiter was serving their coffee and dessert.

"Martina is so tired, and she needs to sleep," he said.

"It must be exhausting to travel with children."

"Yes, but she loves being a mother. She does an excellent job."

"I'm sure you do too, Julian. I can see Felix worships you."

She saw him smile and then his expression turned serious.

"Elena, I must ask you something."

She had an idea of what it was and braced herself for it. "What is it, Julian?"

"Did you tell Stefan you were coming to Austria?"

"No."

"Why not?"

Elena stirred her coffee and scooped up the chocolate foam. "I didn't think it was right to call him after all this time."

"I don't understand."

"Julian, I—"

"Please, Elena. I'm your friend, remember?"

He had a gentle way of coaxing her into opening up to him. "I made a decision many years ago regarding Stefan, which I feel very bad about."

"What do you mean?"

"After I went back to Canada, I stopped writing to him."

"Why?"

"There were many reasons, but one of them was because I moved in with another man. We were together until just recently."

He looked perplexed, and his eyes showed concern. "*That* is the relationship you just finished?"

"Yes, that's right." She licked her spoon and set it down. She no longer had an appetite for dessert.

"Elena, I cannot tell you what to do, but I know Stefan still thinks of you often, especially during this time of year. He never forgot when you were here in Austria with him for Christmas."

His words felt like daggers through her heart. She tried to put on a brave face before responding. "Julian, I never forgot him either, but that was so long ago. He's probably married now, and I'm part of his past. I'm sure he doesn't want to hear from me."

She recalled how she'd abandoned Stefan without explanation. At the time, she had thought little of it, believing she would never see him again anyway. It was something she never forgave herself for, and she realized only now how unbearable her regret was.

Her eyes welled up. She couldn't get over how emotional she was about a brief romance that had happened more than a decade ago. She did not expect Julian to be so relentless in his questioning, nor did she anticipate she would confess to him.

Elena hoped that Julian's silence did not mean he was judging her. She was puzzled as he fumbled in his pocket to retrieve his wallet and asked the waiter for a pen. She guessed he was preparing to settle the bill, but instead he took out a business card and scribbled on it.

"Take this, Elena."

"What is it?" she asked, feeling tears wet her cheeks.

"Trust me—it's not too late for you and Stefan."

*   *   *   *

Elena lay in bed staring at the glowing numbers as they changed on the digital clock next to her. It was two-thirty in the morning. Coffee didn't normally keep her up, and she knew that wasn't the reason she was unable to sleep. Her conversation with Julian had stirred up old memories ... and none of them were good.

She focused on Julian's business card, which she'd placed beside the clock. He had written down Stefan's phone number for her. She reluctantly accepted it, assuring him she would call his friend before flying back home. Somewhere deep within her, though, she was uncertain whether that was the right thing to do. Having recently suffered a breakup, she could not bear a rejection from Stefan right now. Though she wanted to trust Julian, she couldn't just take his word for how Stefan still felt about her.

Elena turned on the lamp and retrieved an envelope from the night table. Inside was a Christmas card accompanied by the final letter she'd received from Stefan. She had probably read it a hundred times since deciding to make the trip to Austria. It was dated the year she returned home. He always typed his letters because he said his penmanship was atrocious. She traced the words of his broken English, which he preferred over writing to her in German. He said it was his way of forcing himself to learn the language. It was the days before computer translators existed, and she suspected he had probably struggled to find the right words with his dictionary. She read the brief block text, perfectly typed and single-spaced.

> *Dear Elena:*
>
> *Thank you for your Christmas card. I am sorry I send my greetings so late.*
>
> *There is nothing new in Austria since I write to you the last time. I work on plans for a big structure in Vienna. It is a bank office that will be ten levels. I get bigger projects now since I am the senior architect with the company.*
>
> *How are you? Are you in love, engaged, or married soon? Do you think we perhaps see each other again?*
>
> *I wish you the very best for the New Year. I hope all your dreams are fulfilled.*
>
> *Best wishes and kisses,*
> *Stefan*

He'd signed his name in blue ink. She read it again, trying to discern whether she misinterpreted the signs so long ago. Stefan was never one to bare his soul, and his letters were no exception. The added challenge of writing in English probably didn't help. Even though it seemed he wanted to see her again, she couldn't determine whether he was serious about pursuing a relationship or was only extending an invitation for another visit. Whatever it was back then, she'd felt she needed something much more tangible than what he offered in his letters.

*   *   *   *

Early morning on Christmas Eve, Elena went skiing. She was leaning toward not contacting Stefan. Under her present circumstances, she didn't think it fair to reconnect with him, no matter how tempting.

She pushed herself on the ski hills and went on a black diamond run for the first time in her life. She was unable to explain her fatalistic move, but she knew she had to do it. When she reached the bottom without suffering any broken limbs, she fell to her knees and kissed the ground. She couldn't remember the last time she'd felt so alive and fearless.

Later that evening, she attended the fireworks in town, as she had every night since first arriving. When she got there, she was surprised to see that the area was practically deserted. When one of the vendors explained that it was too foggy to see the full effects of the fireworks from the valley, she decided to go back to her chalet and watch from her balcony.

Elena had never been alone for Christmas and was feeling a little sorry for herself. She built a fire, poured a glass of wine, and put on a light jacket to step outside. Fortunately, she was located high enough to see above the fog. Less than five minutes later, she heard the first loud boom.

She was in awe as the sky lit up with an array of red and white sun wheels followed by hundreds of streaking fireballs. The snow-covered town was illuminated by all the different colors flying through the air. She felt slightly self-conscious for oohing and aahing on her own, yet she couldn't contain her delight. The bangs and whizzes gave her shivers. During a pause, Elena thought she heard a loud knock from inside the chalet and peered in to see if something had fallen, suspecting a loose log in the fireplace. She didn't see anything unusual.

The fireworks resumed with a loud crack, and numerous rockets pierced the sky. Elena gasped with the splendor of the display, but her attention was again diverted by another series of knocks coming from the interior of the chalet.

What was that noise?

She went in to find out the source and almost jumped out of her skin when she heard several more loud knocks. It was only then that she realized it was someone at her door. She took off her jacket and threw it on the couch.

"One moment, please," she said in German. "Who is it?" She couldn't hear a word because the fireworks were coming to an enthusiastic finale.

"Who is it, please?" The rumble of the explosions was deafening. She waited until it stopped before asking again. "*Wer ist es, bitte?*"

There was a pause before she heard the response. "Stefan."

Elena froze. It was his voice, but she didn't trust her ears, which were still ringing with the sound of fireworks.

"Stefan …," she whispered. "Stefan who?"

"Stefan here to say good night."

She pressed her hands firmly against her chest and felt her heart rate speed up. Elena opened the door. A gust of wind picked up the snow, and it swirled around him. She saw Stefan standing there as if it were ten years earlier.

"So …" She choked up. "It's not Stefan, the big bad wolf?"

"Maybe, but the big bad wolf never knocks."

She found it difficult to breathe. The cold air hit her, yet she felt feverish. He entered and closed the door behind him, then took her in his arms and held her. She immediately teared up. When he broke their embrace, she saw both joy and anguish in his eyes.

Stefan removed his jacket and boots. He had on a blue cotton turtleneck with a pair of black pants. Except for wisps of gray hair by his temples and day-old stubble, he looked the same as the last time she'd seen him. She was in shock.

It was Stefan who led her away from the entrance toward the couch, where they sat in front of the fireplace. He wiped her tears, trailing his fingers down her chin.

"Stefan, how did you know I was here?"

"Julian called me and said he had dinner with you."

"Julian … of course."

"Yes, he said you haven't changed from when we first met you in Thailand." His hand lingered and brushed her wavy hair.

"Stefan ..."

"I think Julian was wrong. You are even more beautiful now."

She blushed. "Stefan, I ..." She couldn't believe how easily he turned her on, even after all this time.

"Julian told me something else."

"What's that?"

"He said he didn't think you would call me before you left. Was he right?" He continued to stroke behind her neck.

"I ..." Elena found it difficult to concentrate.

"Your hair is so soft, just as I remember it."

"Stefan, I—" She felt heat building up between her legs.

"Was Julian right, Elena? Were you going to leave without calling me?"

It was as if he were seducing her into giving him an answer. "Stefan, I don't know ... I had not made up my mind yet." She backed away from his touch.

He looked at her seriously now. "What happened between us? Why did it end?"

She realized now that he had come for an explanation, and how could she blame him? Though she didn't anticipate that Stefan would judge her for choosing another man over him, she was nevertheless disappointed with herself for how she'd ended it. She mustered up the courage to tell him what she should have said so long ago.

"I'm sorry, Stefan." They were the only words she could think of.

"Elena, why are you sorry?"

After a lengthy pause, she knew she had to give him an answer. "I'm sorry I stopped writing. I never meant to end it so abruptly. You deserved better than that." She searched his face for a sign of forgiveness but found none. She felt the intimidation of his eyes on her. "Do you understand my English?"

"Yes, the language is not a problem anymore. I took an English course for six months. It is still not perfect, but it's better than before."

"You're right. It's much improved." She forced a smile to lighten the mood, but he wasn't making it easy for her.

"Elena, why did you never give me your new address?"

"What?" She was confused. "How did you know I moved?"

"I found out when two of my letters came back to me."

"That doesn't make any sense ..."

"They were unopened. Someone had crossed out your address on the envelopes."

"Yes … but … when did you send them?"

"In the New Year, after you went home to Canada."

Elena racked her brain to remember that specific time in her life. Why would she not have received his letters? By all accounts, the rest of her mail had been forwarded properly to Mike's place … unless … She had a sneaking suspicion he had something to do with it. Suddenly, a furious heat swept up her neck and painted her cheeks ruby red.

"Stefan, I never knew you continued to write to me. I should have received your letters, but I didn't … I'm sorry."

He appeared pensive. Elena could not tell whether he was angry or just processing what she told him. Although she would not have put it past Mike to withhold letters from her, she couldn't really blame him for the end of her relationship with Stefan. By then, she had already made her decision.

A part of her wanted to beg Stefan to forgive her and allow them to start over again. When she looked into his eyes, though, she knew he was not ready to hear that. He probably still had questions, and she wasn't sure any of her answers would satisfy him. There was an awkward silence between them.

"Unfortunately, it was much too short a time for us," he said.

His comment ripped her apart. In his few words, she heard regret, sadness, and finality. She silently wept but tried hard to remain composed. "Yes, Stefan, it was too short."

"When do you leave?"

"I fly home a few days after Christmas."

"You are staying here for your entire trip?"

"Yes."

Elena could see he was thinking about something because he furrowed his brow. She was familiar with that expression, which was just one of the many things that endeared him to her.

"Do you have plans for tomorrow?" he asked.

"I … Yes, I was going to go skiing."

"And in the evening?"

"Nothing special." Elena was caught off guard by the change in direction of their conversation.

"I would like to invite you for dinner if you are free."

She was certain he knew she had no other offers. "Are you sure?"

"Of course. I cannot let you leave without at least having dinner with you."

"Okay, Stefan. I would like that very much."

"I will pick you up at five. Is that good?"

"Yes, that's fine … or I'll meet you somewhere if you prefer." She didn't want to inconvenience him, and her fierce independence made her painfully aware of that.

"No, Elena. It will be my pleasure to come and get you. You are again a guest in my country, and I want to make sure you are well taken care of."

"You are too kind," she said, feeling undeserving of his generosity.

He stood up and walked to the door; she followed him. "Just one last question," he said as he put on his coat.

"Yes?"

"You still like classical music, don't you?"

"Uh … yes, of course. Why do you ask?"

"No reason. I wanted to see if I remembered correctly."

"Oh."

"I will see you tomorrow night." He gazed for a brief moment into her eyes, lightly brushing her cheek before letting himself out.

Elena sensed a chill as she looked out the window and saw him walk across the hill to the village. It was surreal to see him again. There was no doubt he had the same effect on her as he had so many years ago. She hugged herself and saw that goose bumps had formed on her arms.

Replaying their conversation in her head after he left, she thought it strange he didn't ask her more questions. Though he wanted to know why she had stopped writing, he didn't pursue the obvious question, which was whether she had met someone else. Did he already know that from what Julian may have told him?

She wanted so much to tell Stefan about that crucial period in her life, how events had spiraled around her, and how she had to make a choice in order to carry on. She didn't need his forgiveness, but she wanted his understanding. Elena now felt that Julian had been wrong. Stefan may never have forgotten her, but based on their brief conversation tonight, she was positive it was too late for them.

She'd heard the sadness in his voice when he spoke of the brief time they'd shared. She had to assume he was also considering how long ago that was, and he probably didn't feel an urge to rehash the past. Now he wanted to take her out for a farewell dinner before she went home. That was just like him. He was always a gentleman—that is, except when it came to the bedroom.

Until she saw him again and felt the intensity of his presence, she had almost forgotten the ferocity of their lovemaking. Now it was coming back to her. She recalled several occasions where he had devastated her body so thoroughly that she was unable to move for hours. Stefan was an anomaly that way. His shy and reserved manner could never have revealed how passionate he was sexually—it was an intoxicating combination for her. She'd never felt so desired by any man, before or since.

*　　　*　　　*　　　*

Christmas Day was a busy one on the slopes, and Elena was on the black diamond run again. She was quite pleased with how her skiing had improved. Though her confidence on the hills was soaring, it was the complete opposite where Stefan was concerned. By the time she returned to the chalet to get ready for their dinner, she felt as if she were having an anxiety attack.

After her shower, she spent almost a half hour deciding what to wear. Like a teenage girl on a first date, she compiled a heap of rejected skirts, pants, and tops on the bed. Nothing fit properly, and she stressed over every detail. Finally, she settled on a simple black knit dress—one of the first things she had tried on. It was understated and showed off her slender figure without being too tight. The last thing she wanted was to wear anything that made her feel uncomfortable—anticipating that being with Stefan was not going to be easy.

It was impossible to prepare for their evening, and she couldn't fool herself by pretending it was just dinner with an old friend. Try as she might, Elena could not stop the internal dialogue. There was a part of her that knew it would be cathartic to reveal everything to Stefan, but that would be for her own benefit, not his. It would be difficult to balance how much she needed to tell him with what he actually wanted to know.

Stefan arrived promptly at five. He was clean-shaven and looked well rested. Wearing a stylish long wool jacket, lightly dusted with snow, he entered and gave her a small peck on the cheek. He stood inside her door and helped her on with her coat before they headed out.

The fresh snowfall sparkled on the ground as they walked to his car outside her chalet. They drove out of the valley, and soon Elena realized they were leaving Bad Gastein altogether.

The very sound of shifting gears was enough to stimulate her. Being so close to Stefan in the car was unnerving, but she admired the way he drove—speed excited her. She turned to watch him and found it impossible not to feel turned on.

She followed Stefan's lead with their conversation. They brought each other up to speed with how their families were, and she discovered they had something in common. Both their fathers had passed away. As with her mom, Stefan's mother was a strong woman who had learned to cope as a widow. Elena recalled Stefan being extremely close to his family, and especially his mom. She saw it as a good sign when a man treated his mother with kindness. It wasn't a hard-and-fast rule, but it usually showed a general respect for women.

She also learned that he had started his own company. His main projects were commercial buildings, and he had secured contracts with some of the major firms in Austria, Germany, and England. She was very proud of him and didn't hesitate to say so. It also explained why his command of the English language had improved so much.

"Do you work a lot with the English?" she asked.

"Yes, I travel to London often each year. Although I have an English-speaking employee, it's important I know the language myself."

"You're almost fluent."

"I still make mistakes, but it helps that I use it more often."

"That's true. I forgot so much of my German until I came back here. It feels wonderful to speak it again."

"I like how you speak German."

"Thank you, but I think your English is better than my German now."

He laughed. "You just need to practice. Maybe you should stay here until you perfect it."

She was rattled by his response. Was he flirting with her or just offering a piece of advice? "I suppose that's a possibility," she said, trying to sound as nonchalant as possible.

"Julian told me you left banking to become a writer."

Elena was amused to find out that Julian had told him so much. "Yes, it's something I've wanted to do since I can remember."

"You wrote even when you were here in Austria last time," he said.

"That's true. I've kept a daily journal since I was a teenager."

"You wrote in it every night, right before you went to bed."

"Wow, you have a good memory."

"Yes, I remember many things about you."

She could not tell if Stefan's words expressed sadness, bitterness, or regret—perhaps a bit of everything.

"What kind of stories do you write?" he asked.

"Erotica."

"Erotica?" He raised his eyebrows.

"Yes."

"These are stories about sex?"

"Not exactly. They're not *about* sex, but they include it."

"Where do you get your ideas from?"

"Different sources, but like most storytelling, some are based on reality and experience—the rest is from my imagination."

"Have you been published?"

"No, not yet."

"What made you decide to write in this … this *category*? Is that the right word?"

"It's not incorrect, but the more accurate term is *genre*. I've been interested in erotica since I first read *Story of O*."

"How old were you then?"

"I was eleven." Elena looked to see if Stefan appeared shocked, but his expression gave nothing away.

"So it's been a part of you almost all your life," he said.

"I suppose so. I always thought I could write good stories, but practicality won out, and I went into a safe profession instead—safe financially, that is."

"That's why you chose banking?"

"Yes, I found the job not long after I got home from traveling. I needed to make some money but never imagined I would do it for so many years."

"Can you earn a living as a writer?"

"I hope so, although it might take awhile. Most writers keep their day jobs, but I was unable to do both. It helps that there is a large market for erotica right now—I aim to capitalize on that."

"I think it's good that you write."

"Oh? Why is that?"

"I do not see you as a banker. You are much too—"

"Too what?"

"Too sensual."

She thought it was a strange thing to say. "I'm not sure I know what you mean."

At that moment, he made a left turn and accelerated onto the autobahn. Elena had presumed they would be dining at one of the other ski resorts, but after driving for over thirty minutes, she now saw that they were going into the city of Salzburg. Stefan was an extremely fast driver, yet she felt at ease with him as he changed gears to keep pace with traffic moving at a steady 150 kilometers.

Her curiosity got the better of her. "May I ask where we're going?"

"Yes, you may ask, but I won't tell you," he said.

"Oh …" She was taken aback by his response.

"It's a surprise. I think you will like it."

Charmed by his playfulness, she relaxed. "Okay, I'm looking forward to it, then." She guessed that Stefan remembered she loved to be surprised.

"Good."

"You were saying …" Elena was feeling less apprehensive about their evening and finding herself enjoying their conversation.

"Yes, what I mean about you being too sensual … How can I explain it?" He sounded extremely comfortable with the language. "I see different professions for different types of people. Banking is not for you."

"Really? Why do you say that?"

"It is a very regulated industry. Am I correct?"

"Yes … there is not much room for creativity if that's what you mean."

"Right. Even in my profession, I consider myself to be innovative, but there are still many rules I must follow."

"Of course. Otherwise, a building could collapse. It's important you have standards."

"Yes, with banking too. You are dealing with people's money—their livelihoods. It is important work, but I do not see you in it."

"You don't think I can follow rules?"

"No, it's not that. I just think you need more freedom to express yourself." He paused as he came upon an intersection. "I remember you as someone who feels so much, and banking is a profession of the head, not the heart. I cannot explain it in English so well, but I hope you understand."

She did. "Yes, writing makes me feel alive. I couldn't say that about my work at the bank, especially not during the last few years."

"Then you've made the right decision to leave your job, and I predict you will be successful as a writer."

"Thank you. I appreciate your saying that."

"Maybe someday you will write a story about us."

She immediately felt flushed. "About us?"

"You said you write erotic stories, right?"

"Yes."

"You and I have a good story to tell, but …"

Elena followed his eyes as he drove into a parking lot. "But what?"

"But the ending has yet to be written." He pulled into a spot and turned off the ignition.

She was left guessing at what he meant.

They had arrived, but she had no clue where they were. They were parked near a spectacular property consisting of multiple buildings, unlike anything she had ever seen before.

"Stefan, where are we?"

"We are at Stiftskirche St. Peter. The English translation is St. Peter's Abbey." He pointed to the church in front of them. "That is St. Peter's Church, where it is believed that Christianity was first introduced to Austria."

"That's remarkable."

"Yes, the neighborhood here is the oldest quarter of Salzburg, and this is the most ancient monastery in the German-speaking world. Benedictine monks have lived here for centuries."

"Amazing."

"Come, I'll show you."

They got out of the car. A gentle snowfall had just started. Stefan led her by the elbow toward a courtyard, where she saw the grandeur of the surrounding structure. The steeple of St. Peter's church jutted out from among the buildings.

"The church was built at the beginning of the eighteenth century," he explained. "The interior is quite magnificent with its high marble pillars and a fresco ceiling."

She was awestruck by the exterior beauty of it. "What style of architecture is this?"

"You tell me," he said.

Elena recalled how Stefan had piqued her interest in the imperial architecture of the Austrian Empire. She had learned that the country had a confection of structures ranging from the Gothic period, with St. Stephen's Cathedral, to modern-day innovations, which stood in stark contrast to the historic buildings. Despite her limited knowledge, she still loved a challenge. "Hmm, I have to make a wild guess."

"All right."

"I'm going to say ... Baroque?"

"That's very good." He seemed genuinely pleased that she knew the answer. "This church was originally constructed in the Romanesque period, then completely renovated with Baroque elements. The altars of the church are done in Late-Baroque, otherwise known as the Rococo style."

Elena squealed with delight. "I'm shocked I guessed correctly—I amaze myself sometimes!"

"See, you did learn something from when you were last here."

"Yes, I remembered the design of the Schönbrunn Palace. Did that also have both Baroque and Rococo elements?"

"It did. You're absolutely right."

Elena was proud of her accurate recollection. "Are we going in the church?"

"No, maybe later. Now we're going to the oldest restaurant in Europe."

"Really?"

"Yes, Stiftskeller St. Peter."

"St. Peter's Cellar. How old is it?"

"It was opened in eight-oh-three."

Her jaw dropped. "We're talking about the ninth century, right?"

"Yes."

"It's hard to fathom the history of this place." She was still in disbelief. "Canada is such a young country by comparison."

Stefan nodded and guided her in the direction of one of the arched doorways. "I remember you loved food and music, correct?"

"Yes, to both."

"Good, I have arranged a concert for us while we have dinner."

"Nice. How did you manage that?"

"The owners are friends of mine, and my company has done some work here," he said, pausing to add, "I hope you like Mozart."

"Of course!"

"You probably already know Salzburg is filled with the history of him."

"Yes, I visited his house and museum the last time."

"Then you may already be familiar with his association to this place."

"No, I'm not aware of it."

"Mozart's Mass in C Minor premiered here at St. Peter's Church in 1783. His wife, Constance, sang the soprano solos at the performance. So, in keeping with the Mozart theme, we will be having dinner in the Wolfgang Parlor, one of the private dining rooms."

"Okay." Elena took a breath. "Now I'm really impressed."

She stopped in her tracks and put her hand on his arm. "Stefan, this is the nicest thing anyone has done for me in a long time." Turning to look at him, she stood on her toes and tentatively gave him a kiss on the cheek. "Thank you."

He glared at her, then grabbed her by the lapels and pulled her close. "Damn it, Elena, you don't know how much I've missed you."

He shocked her with his uncharacteristic declaration. His face was impossible to read.

Surrounded by history, Elena saw the ghosts of her past coming back to haunt her. "Stefan, I—"

He kissed her in the deserted courtyard of the abbey. It was snowing more heavily now, but not even the night chill could soothe the fire growing inside her.

She was weak from his mouth on hers and thankful he was holding her up, as her legs felt like they might buckle beneath her. He was gentle at first, and then he pressed harder. She suddenly had a flashback to the fiery dominance of his slow and deliberate lovemaking. She allowed his need to bruise her lips and invade her with his tongue.

His hunger for her was palpable. She responded in kind, desperate to satisfy the lust that had been growing for him since first laying eyes on him again.

It was Stefan who stepped back first. "Elena, you touched me deeply when I first met you. I thought I would forget you, but I never did. I can't explain it."

"Stefan ..." Elena felt herself choking up. "I made a big mistake. I wanted so much to stay in Austria with you, but I was waiting for you to ask me—I was afraid you didn't want me to stay."

"You only gave me a taste of you the last time. I wanted so much more."

He hugged her against him tightly, and her heart swelled with the words she had always wanted to hear him say.

"I'm so sorry, Stefan. I never knew that."

He reawakened an ache she had known of for years. In the final months with Mike, when things were unbearable, she'd sensed an itch she couldn't scratch. Often it was a deep sadness, but every now and then, she felt the sting of doubt and regret. She was never able to pinpoint its origin until now—it was the pain of her decision to let Stefan go.

"Julian told me you are a free woman now. Is that true?"

"Yes."

"When did your relationship end?"

"It happened at the beginning of this year, but it was over long before that."

He looked at her with tenderness in his eyes. "I wanted so much to kiss you yesterday when I first saw you. It took everything I had not to."

"Oh, Stefan ..."

He held her hands in his. "I had no idea how fragile you might be. I didn't want to take advantage of you."

"You are ever the gentleman."

"Trust me—I didn't want to be. But if I had kissed you, it would not have ended there."

Elena had butterflies in her stomach. When his lips met hers again, he was unhurried and thorough. A storm brewed between them, and it was both painful and pleasurable for her to rediscover him. The yearning she felt for him was exquisite.

As difficult as it was, Elena broke from his kiss to ask a question that had been eating away at her. "Stefan, you said you wrote me two letters that were returned to you."

"Uh-huh." He moved to nuzzle her neck.

Elena felt heat between her legs but reluctantly pursued the question. "Did you stop writing me because I didn't give you my new address?"

He gazed into her eyes, and she saw pain in them.

"Elena, when your letters stopped coming and I didn't have your correct address, I thought it was your way of telling me it's over."

She hung her head, afraid to continue, but she had to know. "Stefan, what did you write in those last letters you sent me?"

"It is not so important anymore."

"Please, Stefan, it's important to me."

He took an extra breath before speaking. "I wrote that I wanted to see you again, that ..."

"Yes?" Her heart pounded out of her chest.

"Elena, do you really want to hear this?"

"I need to know."

"All right ... I wrote that I hoped you would come back to Austria—and to me."

She could not contain her tears. Even though there was no point in grieving the past, it was still a bitter pill for her to swallow. If only she had not moved in with Mike ... If only she had received Stefan's letters sooner ... If only ... She lamented all the years gone by.

"Oh, Stefan—so much time has passed."

"I know," he said.

"It's not too late for us?"

"Elena, I kept my feelings for you inside for much too long. When Julian told me you were here, I could not stay away. I have missed you for ten years, for ten Christmases ..."

She heard the desire in his voice. "Stefan ..."

"No, listen to me. I don't want to be with you just for your holiday. I want you with me for this Christmas, and the next, and every other Christmas after. Do you understand?"

Elena stopped crying long enough to answer. "Yes."

He held her tearstained face, and she heard what sounded like a sigh of relief emanate from him. When his mouth found hers, she opened up to him with abandon. It felt so different now that she knew he had wanted her all along. She could only define it as the feeling of two lost souls finding one another again. They kissed for what seemed like an eternity, yet it was still not long enough for her.

Stefan abruptly moved back, held her by the shoulders, and gave her a stern look.

"What is it?" she asked, startled by his change in expression.

"Elena, we have to get going. You don't want to miss dessert, do you?"

She playfully punched him. "Stefan, you've really improved your sense of humor!"

"I remember you liked to laugh."

"Yes, that's true," she said, sniffling and wiping her face.

"Let's go." He took her arm and looped it around his. "Mozart and *Nockerl* await."

"Nockerl? You mean the soufflé made famous here in Salzburg?"

"Yes."

"Now I'm really excited. How did you know I always wanted to try it?"

He smiled. "I didn't."

When Elena had booked her trip, she'd thought she was returning to a country that captured her heart the first time. She now realized that it wasn't an affinity for Austria that drew her back; it was the special bond with the Austrian who lived there.

about the author

EDEN BAYLEE remembers hiding under the blankets with a flashlight and reading an erotic novel. It was past her bedtime—she was eleven.

Since then, she has continued to read and write erotica. Equipped with an active imagination, few inhibitions, and a passion for words, she is fortunate to have experienced much of what she writes about, and she integrates many of her favorite things into her stories.

An introvert by nature and an extrovert by design, Ms. Baylee is most comfortable at home with her laptop, surrounded by books, music, and a cup of homemade chai tea.

She is an online Scrabble junkie and social networking enthusiast, but she really needs to get out more often!

Fall into Winter is Ms. Baylee's first book.

Take a sensual journey with her at www.edenbaylee.com

LaVergne, TN USA
10 January 2011
211883LV00001B/7/P